Feathers Fall

Ben Wise

www.ben-wise.com

ISBN: 0994194757
ISBN-13: 978-0-9941947-5-6

This is a work of fiction. Names, characters, businesses, places, events and incidents either are the products of the author's imagination or used in a fictitious manner. Any resemblance to actual persons, living or dead, or actual events is purely coincidental.
I promise…

Acknowledgements

Thanks as always go to Schwartzie, who once again offered far too much of her time to fix my shortcomings as a writer and turn this story into something actually readable.

This is a story about her

Tuesday Morning December 9th 1997

I'd never have expected I'd find anybody down there. It was my spot, my own secret hide away, that one place that everybody has when you need to get away from everybody and everything. For most people it's as simple as a bedroom, a quiet room or anywhere outdoors. Mine, rather specifically, happened to be a half hour hike through the mountainous national park near my house.

It was my somewhat humble opinion that my place was the most beautiful place around; my own little glen tucked in the forest not far from my house. Peacefully filled by the clamour of hundreds of birds, my retreat was altogether devoid of the outside world. Everything in this little valley lived in the shadow of Aerie Falls; an anaemic waterfall that barely trickled over the rocky outcrop that loomed overhead. What little water made it over the falls fell into a small icy pool, which then ran down the valley to become

Figfall Creek as it continued through the forest. The creek's name apparently came from its destructive nature toward the figs that grew along it. Maybe it came from the one massive fig that grew crooked over the creek, more horizontal than vertical, defeated despite its size. If one were to look down the creek however at all the other figs that appeared to be having no problems whatsoever, it would appear as if the figs were winning the battle decisively. The trees grew so heavy that sunlight almost couldn't pierce the foliage, leaving the valley freezing cold and in almost constant shadow.

I'd go down there, stick my feet in the freezing water and relax. There were a few good trees to sit under beside the pool and all my favourite pastimes included spending time under them. Many pages have been flipped here, and more have been stared at blankly for hours as my thoughts wandered elsewhere. Frequently I'd find myself staring at the same page I'd started hours ago. Considering things, I used to be a lot more creative in past years. Drawing, painting etc. The usual creative outlets. I don't know why not so much these days. I'm not sure I even cared that that had slipped away from me.

On that day, it was summer, a Tuesday, and two weeks into the school holidays, post Year 11. I was already bored. I had the day off from my part time job, and since everyone else I knew didn't, I had nothing to do, at least not until later that night when there were plans to get together to watch movies at my place. The Lost World had recently been released on video and my friends and I had planned a Jurassic Park marathon at my place, which, given the fact I held an almost obsessive love of dinosaurs that had remained since I was a little kid, meant I was quite excited about the evening.

I had stocked up on Jolt and headed down to the falls with a tattered copy of The Catcher in the Rye in my backpack expecting to burn the day away. I always went alone. This place felt like my little secret. I expected to be alone. That was the plan. I'd never seen anybody else there. Which surprises me a little, come to think about it. It wasn't as if it was difficult to find and it wasn't exactly off the beaten track. Hell, the falls even had its own sign and walking track and everything. While the walking track may cover a fair distance, I was hardly the kind of person willing to put up with a difficult hike. I'd done my life's share of hiking as a scout and I liked that place exactly because it involved none of that.

Then, that day, she was there. The first time I had seen another person there. And the best plans in life collapsed. Her name was Kate. Kate Rees, though I didn't remember that at the time. It could have been that I was more surprised at my own surprise at seeing somebody there than anything else. I knew we went to school together and she was in my grade. And that's about all I knew about her. She hung out with one of the cool groups and the chances of them mixing with my more nerdy group were somewhere between sweet and fuck all. Usual high school cliquey shit. Perhaps not quite the Hollywood cliché, but let's not lie, it was close enough.

And she was beautiful. Really beautiful. Way out of my league kind-of beautiful. It was only because of my massive crush on her friend Amy that I had never given her much notice before. Crush blindness; she could have been right in front of me and I'd have never paid her any attention. Even so, I knew, realistically, it wasn't as if a geek like me had a chance with either of them.

That day, I paid attention. She had dark coffee brown hair so ridiculously stunning it seemed iridescent in the sun. Impossibly so, I thought. My mind refused to believe that real brown hair could ever get so deep and vibrant. I was wrong, but that comes later. Either way, I freely admit she sold that colour. She always had it tied back the same way, loose and carefree with rough bangs hanging from her face. I also happened to notice that she had, at least from this young male's perspective, the perfect body. I mean, she wasn't athletic or wafer thin or ridiculously curvy. She was perfectly nice. Beautiful. It feels somewhat strange now describing her from a purely physical perspective. Before was different.

Kate was one of those dream girls that I, perhaps because of my immaturity, had instantly written off. She seemed so perfect that I'd automatically attributed to her a fatal flaw, a 'necessary' imperfection, to make her seem real. I could only have assumed a girl that looked as good she did, and kept the company she did, was all beauty and nothing else. Surely, I thought, that must have been her flaw. And, for a geek like me, hollow beauty was an empty promise. I would tell myself how much I treasured knowledge in my own twisted superiority complex, and so I felt that any girl I would be interested in should do the same. Knowledge was the only thing truly beautiful, I thought. How I rationalised my crush on Amy, despite these thoughts I had no idea. I was a stupid and immature young boy. The reality was that I didn't know a thing about Kate.

And I couldn't have been more wrong about what is truly beautiful. I would find that out in time. And I couldn't have been more wrong about her. If I claimed this story to be mine, that would be a lie. No, this is hers.

You see, at the time, two months and a lifetime ago, as she stood facing the falls with her back turned to me, she happened to be manoeuvring the barrel of a hunting rifle in front of her face. While it was only

5

small rifle, reminding me a lot of my grandfather's old .22 rifle that he kept despite the recent gun ban, she appeared to be struggling to reach the trigger while aiming the barrel beneath her chin.

Now, most people coming across this situation might have reacted a little more intelligently, helpfully even. Perhaps offered some suggestion of how much life was worth living or something else meaningful to make her think twice. Perhaps they might have told her how much her family loved her and would miss her if she were to do something stupid. Anything at all that would convince her not to go through with it. Instead, I reached deep my well of beautiful knowledge and came forth with this gem:

"You know, a .22 isn't much of a bullet. It probably won't be enough to kill you, probably leave you brain dead or something."

She, startled by my sudden presence, reacted accordingly. The gun went off with a pop. Something went whizzing past my ear. I'm undoubtedly lucky that my unexpected appearance so shocked her that the gun slipped. I'm also probably lucky that she missed shooting me instead. She kept the burn on her neck for over a week and I'm sure that to this day I was the only person aware of the cause.

"Shit!" she screamed.

And then we were staring at each other, neither sure what to do next. Her eyes blurred red yet, despite the metres between us, they looked deep into mine asking questions I wasn't sure I could answer. The seconds ticked. Eventually her hand dropped.

"Are you ok?" I asked.

Which was a far better question to ask. She nodded. It came out slowly at first as she took her time to think about it.

"Yeah, I think I'll be ok."

I closed the distance between us.

"Let me take that," I said softly, reaching out toward her.

She peered up at me with a guilty expression and then handed over the rifle.

"You sure you'll be ok?"

"Yeah, it's over now."

"What brought you out to this place?"

She looked at the gun in my hand. I looked at the gun in my hand. We shared a moment of awkwardness.

"Apart from that."

"I just walked, you know? Walked until I'd walked as far as I could," she said, shrugging.

I'd never thought of it like that before. I laughed at the irony. I had kept the place to myself to hold onto some selfish desire for exclusiveness and yet for her it was simply a convenient place to step off the road. It didn't make much sense to keep it a secret anymore. There is something to be said about giving up secrets to somebody. But secrets need a reason to exist and mine evaporated into insignificance when measured against her near fatal presence there that day. I still hesitated. It was hard to give up on the idea. Or the ideal.

"It's nothing much. I suppose it's silly, really. Do you believe in having a secret place? You know. A place all of your own that nobody else knows about where you can go to get away from people. This place was mine. I like to come here and spend time alone."

At first, she looked at me as if I was crazy. Her lips pursed in thought.

"And I've come and spoilt your secret," she said. "I'm sorry. I guess we both have secrets to keep today. Will you tell anybody?"

I thought about it briefly. I should have. I knew I should have. But sometimes reason isn't reasoned.

"No."

Her whole body relaxed. She placed a hand on my shoulder and leant into me.

"Thank you," she whispered as she leant back and smiled, her face, despite her glistening eyes, beamed with apparent happiness. "I promise I won't tell anybody about your secret place. It's really nice." She nodded her head as she looked around. "I can see why you like it."

She took a seat under a willow that overhung where the pool flowed into the creek and looked up at me, knees tucked under her chin and her feet an inch out of the water.

"Stay with me a while?" she asked.

I sat down next to her. Not too close mind you. Because what was the appropriate distance to maintain? I wasn't sure. My experience with girls up until that point was limited enough, but suicidal girls? What was I supposed to do? No idea. They don't teach this stuff. So I did what anybody else would do. I pretended as if the problem didn't exist. I took my shoes off and stuck my feet in the water. She responded with a flashed look of curiosity and then, and to my surprise, followed my lead, taking her shoes off and dipping her feet in the water.

"Oh shit! That's freezing!" she said, holding her feet above the water.

I laughed.

"You did that on purpose," she said, pushing me playfully.

"This is what I do every time I come down here."

"Bull."

"Truth."

Gingerly, she inched her feet back into the water.

"I suppose it's not so bad," she said, tentatively.

"See?"

"I'm lying, it's bloody freezing," she retorted, poking her tongue out at me.

"Sorry."

"Don't be."

"I was lying." I poked my tongue back at her.

"Bite me."

"Don't tempt me."

That earned me a giggle. We fell silent, both leaning back against the tree while we aimlessly stared into the water. We both understood.

"Do you want something to drink?" she asked, breaking the silence.

I reached for my backpack. "Oh, I'm sorted," I said, flashing one of the bottles of cola at her like the innocent fool I was. "Want one?"

She shook her head and laughed before opening her backpack and pointing to a half-empty bottle of vodka inside. What I also saw, however, standing out so obviously, was the small box of bullets beside it.

"This might be a terrible question to ask, but what did you need the whole box for?"

Her eyes followed mine to the box. She picked it up out of the bag and shook it, getting a brief rattle.

"I don't think there's many left. Fair point though, I will admit to not entirely thinking things through," she responded, taking a swig of vodka.

She passed the bottle to me. It was my turn to act timidly. Being both nerdy and terribly uncool, I had never crossed alcohol before. At least, not a spirit like this. I suspect the sip of Granddad's horrible tasting beer as a kid at Christmas doesn't count. Therefore, I didn't have a clue what to expect. I took a big swig and promptly spat it out all over myself. Kate burst out laughing beside me.

"A vodka virgin?"

"What's it to you?" I responded, a little sharper than intended.

"Nothing, nothing. I think it's cute that I popped your vodka cherry."

My vodka cherry? That was one way to look at it. And that's why you weren't cool Sam, I thought to myself. I took another swig, the biggest I could manage and handed her the bottle back. It went down a little easier that time. A little. She sat there, bottle in hand, still giggling at me.

"Impressive. We'll turn you into an alcoholic in no time."

"We?" I asked.

"The royal we," she responded.

"Since you're a princess?"

That sent her into an uncontrolled giggle fit. Then she stopped suddenly, sighed and went back to staring into the water. She avoided my gaze at first, as we continued to pass the bottle back and forth, wordlessly. Whatever was on her mind, it seemed to weigh heavily on her. While alcohol probably wasn't the best idea all things considered, I was glad to watch her demeanour shift the more we drank. She relaxed further against our shared tree trunk, visibly more relieved.

It turns out, however, that neither of us could hold our alcohol. Somewhere near the bottom of the bottle, I decided it might be a good idea to reach across her and grab the bullets out of her bag. My rather innocent intention, drunkenly distorted, was to play around with them. I managed instead, in the most graceless of fashions, to slip and thus ended face down in her lap. Frozen with embarrassment, I lay stuck in horror.

"You know, most boys start with a date and a movie first," she said bemusedly.

"Oh shit," I half mumbled, flailing about as I tried to right myself. "I'm so sorry!"

"It's quite ok," she said, grinning subtlety. "You know, I have these things called hands which are quite capable of grabbing things if only you ask first."

"Bite me," I responded, noticing for the first time the subtle freckling brushed on under those crystal green eyes, so subtle that they weren't visible until I'd gotten close. Hell, she was beautiful. We sat there, eyes fixed.

"Like I said, don't tempt me."

She gazed back, a moment held. She was so much more beautiful this close. My eyes slipped from hers, down her cheeks to her soft lips. I couldn't tell if she was blushing or flushed from the alcohol.

Then, perhaps as we realised that we'd already spent too long staring at each other and having fully considered the implications of such, we both turned away, the moment over, nervous smiles shared and a return to aimlessly staring at the icy pool.

"You ever used one of those before?" she asked.

"What?"

"The gun."

"No."

"Pass it here."

Naturally, I hesitated. Wouldn't you?

"I promise I won't do anything stupid. I'm fine. The feeling is over. I promise."

And naturally, I still hesitated. She flashed another smile to me, as if to explain that she understood. There was pain still written on her face, but at least her lips sold the truth. So, naturally, I folded. I handed her the gun. In hindsight, it was a stupid thing to do and I should never have capitulated but at least to my relief all she did was load it before passing it back to me. I held it like a fool who had never held a gun before because I was a fool who had never held a gun before.

"Point it at something other than me!" she said, ducking her head out of the way quickly as she pushed the gun barrel toward the forest. She shook her head disapprovingly. "Call it."

"Call it?"

"You need to call out what you're aiming at."

"Ok. On the tree that's fallen over the creek, there's a big patch of moss growing in the middle almost. Can you see it?"

"Sure. You reckon you can hit that from here? Good luck," she said, unconvinced.

"You don't think I can?"

"Just shoot the damn thing."

So I took aim and tried my best not to look stupid. Finger on the trigger. Squeeze carefully.

"So, um, do you have a girlfriend?" she half mumbled.

Pop!

"Shit!"

I almost dropped the gun. Beside me, she was laughing a curious mix between embarrassed giggles and outright to the point of tears laughter. The tree remained firmly unscathed. I remained firmly drowning in my awkwardness.

"I'm stirring. I'll take that as a no."

I handed her back the gun, before I ended up hurting myself. Still unsure what it was best to respond with here. Was it not obvious? I mean, could she not see me? Pasty white, skinny, nerd with the glasses and all.

"Look at me. Do I look like I have a girl?"

She shrugged and reloaded the gun. "I don't see why not?"

Pop! A dull thud and a brief puff of splintered wood showed that she hit the mark. She blew the smoke off the barrel to show off. If I squinted, I could barely see the new hole that had appeared in the rotting tree trunk.

"It's hard to if you hit it or not."

She rolled her eyes. "Wait here."

She stepped down the creek with the vodka bottle in hand. Stopping about fifteen metres away, next to a large rock that jutted out next to the creek, she looked back at me, took the final swig of vodka, wiped her lips and then balanced the bottle on the rock. It didn't slip my mind that upon her return she sat down somewhat closer than before. It also didn't slip my mind that I seemed quite a lot more comfortable with the idea.

"Well, what are you waiting for, shoot it," she said as she gave me playful push.

I aimed. Waited. Looked at her again, expecting another question.

"What…?" She laughed, waving off the expectations. "Shoot! Hurry up already."

Pop! Dirt puffed up from the rock the bottle stood on, but the bottle itself remained.

"Ok then, so tell me, if no girlfriend, who's your crush?"

I sat there stupefied. The window for denial ran straight past me and never bothered looking back. I still gave it a shot. Silly boy.

"I, ah, um, yeah, don't have one."

I would have had better luck convincing her I was a girl.

"Oh yeah, of course," she replied with a sarcastic eye roll before she slipped into a friendly smile. "Haven't I already promised to keep your secrets today?"

She loaded another bullet, took aim at the empty bottle, and waited for an answer.

"Well? Hurry up already, this thing is heavy."

"I kind of, maybe, had my eye on Amy."

Pop! The vodka bottle exploded.

"See, that wasn't so hard," she said. Her face twisted in thought as my answer sunk in. "Amy huh? You and everyone else, it seems. She certainly is a cutie. But let's be honest here. Like, I'd hate to be the one to ruin your fantasies, but she would chew you up and spit you out."

"What do you mean?"

"Ah, well, Amy can seem a little cold at times. Not a bad person, don't get me wrong. She can be a tough nut to crack, tis all. As a couple of people have already found out the hard way these holidays." She added with a brief giggle. "Three guys and one girl, if I remember correctly. Hah, she can certainly have a way with people. She's a good friend, but when it comes to the relationship stuff, she's never seemed interested. If you want my advice, for you own sanity, look but don't touch."

Which I didn't think much of, considering I never expected anything to become of my little crush anyway.

"What about you?" I asked.

She flashed me a look of uncertainty. It took me a moment to figure out why.

"Um, I mean, do you have a boyfriend?"

Her expression dropped with a quick shake of her head. A sore subject? I let it drop. She followed up with a quick half-smile, shuffled a little closer and leant her ahead against my shoulder.

"Let's not ruin the moment."

That was the first of many lessons Kate would teach me. Life is about moments. Moments like these. The experiences, the people, the constant desire to touch and question and live to experience, the flash of a smile and the conversation that seems to last forever, the hurtful word said in haste and the way the girl beside you leant her head on your shoulder and changed your world forever.

Tuesday Afternoon December 9th 1997

The more we sat together, the better it felt. I was still nervous, certainly, but there was a certain sort of comfort in that feeling. A simple shared moment. The minutes passed wordless. There was something about her that made things ok.

"Can I have one of your bottles of cola?" Kate eventually asked.

With everything so serious, her question seemed so... I don't know, minor, simplistic, out of place. The tension was different. Relaxed. Over. I handed her one from my bag.

"They're probably a little warm now."

She shrugged, cracked it open and took a sip.

"Bloody hell that's sweet. What's in this, straight sugar?"

I laughed. "What, did I pop your Jolt Cola cherry?"

"Hah, yes you did. And I rather enjoyed it."

Kate stood up, a little more wobbly this time. She used my shoulder to steady herself. She then sculled the whole bottle of Cola, finishing it rather ungracefully. At that we both laughed.

She took a deep bow, and, in the same movement, went to fill up the empty bottle with water from the pool. Then she slipped, landing unceremoniously butt first into the creek. That time, as she sat glowering in those few inches of freezing water, I was the only one laughing for quite a while. I eventually got a smile to slip past her scowling lips. A smile that grew into laughter as she, resolved to her misfortune, took the opportunity to fill the bottle up with water.

She stood up, kicked the icy water playfully at me, then went and placed the water filled bottle on same tree.

"Try shooting it standing up," she said as she walked back to me.

"You just want to push me in."

She looked away as she struggled to hide her grin.

'Two more bullets left," she said, loading the gun and handing it to me again.

Pop! I missed again.

She shook her head at me. "Well I guess that bottle lives to fight another day."

"But there's still one bullet left?"

"Keep it," she said, dropping the bullet in the palm of my right hand and curling my fingers around it. "Consider it a memory of our day together. It's time for me to head home."

She then slipped the gun from my left hand and slid it into her bag. She probably could tell from my reluctance that I still wasn't sure I should be handing it over.

"If I don't get it back before my father notices it's missing, he'll kill me." She leant up to me and wrapped her arms around me in a gentle hug. "I'll be ok, promise. I won't do anything stupid. We should do this again sometime."

"Sure," I said, disappointed to feel her arms unwrap from me.

She then pushed me into the pool, twisted on the spot and walked away. She peeked over her shoulder only long enough to let me see the giant grin on her face one last time as she walked away.

"Bye."

Then she was gone. And as the freezing water seeped into places freezing water quite honestly doesn't belong, I realised that my expectations of enjoying tonight at the movies with my friends would pale against the time I'd spent with her.

I can't say how long I sat there thinking about it. Sat there thinking about her. I kept telling myself nothing could become of it. Just look at me, I told myself. She was set to become just another unanswered question. And no matter how much knowledge I gained, I'd never have an answer.

And so, sitting in the icy pool as I was, depressed at it all, I decided to do something completely out of character; I resolved to do something about it. Only, as slow as I was to come to that conclusion, she had already long disappeared.

"Shit." I swore at myself as I jumped out of the pool. Freezing water ran uncomfortably down the inside of my pants as I grabbed my bag and raced off out of the valley. Surely, I thought, she couldn't have gotten that far ahead. I hoped, more like.

The further I ran without catching up to her, the more I realised that a) I'd missed another opportunity and b) I should have done a lot more exercise.

As penance for my foolish hope, I jogged the rest of the way back through the forest. The track itself exited at a grassy field, a park that was once popular with local families but these days well overrun. I saw her as I left the forest and stumbled into the grassy field. She was already on the other side of the field from me, moments away from her parked hatchback. I paused, momentarily defeated and out of breath, as she walked casually to the driver's door. A quiet voice in my head pointed out the fact that she could drive was neat. Another voice cut in rather more urgently, drowning out the first with the words 'She's getting away!'

I ran across the field, yelling and waving my arms, looking idiotic no doubt, trying anything that might get her attention. I made it halfway across the field as the car starting reversing out of the parking spot. Three quarters of the way across the field as she crunched into gear. I vaulted the low chain fence into the parking area just as her car reached the end of the street. I was so close. So damn close. Dejected, I turned away, exhausted and struggling to catch my breath.

I barely had the energy to jump out of the way when she almost reversed over me. She opened her door and stood half in, half out of the car.

"I almost didn't see you!"

I only managed to huff and puff a response. Of course, as soon I got my breath back the nerves kicked in, leaving me as speechless.

"I, ah…I…"

She looked down at me, amused.

"Me and my friends are watching a few movies at my place tonight. Starts at seven. We're going to watch Jurassic Park and The Lost World. I was wondering, um, if you wanted to join us, maybe?"

It came out in a flurry of words. She blinked a few times; her cheeks flushed as she spent a few seconds considering my question. It was an intolerable wait.

"Yeah, I'll be there," she said, beaming.

"It's ok…" I started apologizing. "Wait. Yes?" It took a moment to sink in.

"Yeah, I'll come. Why do you sound so surprised? It sounds like fun. And by the way, thanks for the wet car seat," she joked. "But I need to get home, so I'll see you then."

She ducked back into her car, shut the door, and started to drive off. Five metres down the road her car stopped and she opened her door. Leaning out, she looked at me sheepishly.

"I have no idea where you live."

"Oh yeah, that would probably help."

I gave her my address and directions, all the while thinking to myself how stupid I was not to have thought of that.

"See you!"

Long after her car had disappeared around a corner, I was still standing there, uncertain whether I had imagined what had happened, or if this was all some perverse dream. I had to remind myself not to get too far ahead of things. It was just movies with friends. As if that was going to stop my imagination. It was already off playing in the clouds. I had to keep dragging myself back to earth.

One curious thought did cross my mind. What about Amy? It strangely felt like I was throwing her away, as if all ones thoughts of a crush actually meant something. Can you cheat on a crush? Perhaps it was more like cheating on myself. As if I had been selling this fairy tale to myself the whole time, knowing it was a lie yet still I ignored the lie to please myself. And why? Why do we lie to ourselves like that? Desire? Hope? Fantasy? The pertinent question though was had I swapped one unlikely fantasy for another? I figured as much. Did that worry me? Not one bit. Perhaps that was simply the warm and fuzzy feeling of a new crush building the foundations of a new fairy tale.

How I came to be staring at the ceiling above my bed, I have no clue. I assume I rode home, though I don't remember a moment of the journey. That's quite an impressive feat considering the maze of streets between home and that park. Less impressive was the fact that I was still in my wet clothes. On my bed. More concerned with the ceiling paint than the water seeping into my doona. Shit. The fantasy scored its first win against me. The doona hadn't gotten too damp thankfully, so it wasn't all bad. I did feel stupid though.

I met with my closest friends Zach and Lizzie at Corner Pizzeria at six. Zach and Lizzie were dating at that moment, but those two were serial daters. They had been dating on and off since the age of twelve, at least five or six times now. I'd lost count. And with those two, it can be hard to tell whether they're on or off at times. At almost thirteen months together this time around, they were setting a new record for themselves but I'd noticed that the wagon was getting a little shaky. Corner Pizzeria was our go to meeting place. We'd always head there before doing anything else. Which was somewhat annoying tonight, since it meant heading out just so I could head home again, but tradition was tradition. And at sixteen, I had to take advantage of the fact that riding my bike to the pizza shop was about as close as I could get to afford getting pizza delivered. At least the place was close.

All the take-away places around town were terrible, but Corner Pizzeria was notorious. We firmly believed though that if any of the food around here was going to kill us, we might as well make the most of it. It helped that since Lizzie and I worked there part time we had a pretty good idea of what to avoid. That and the owner sometimes gave us free stuff if we stayed long enough. Free stuff always made for a winning argument.

I was late and I'm normally never late. The afternoon had left me distracted and unable to focus. All sorts of scenarios kept running through my head. Things I could say, things that might happen. It was all about her. How I managed to shower and dress, I had no idea. All afternoon all I had managed to do was lie in bed – minus doona – and stare at the ceiling. There was a constant voice in my head telling me I was being irrational, it's nothing special, it's just a night with friends; she probably won't even show up. It wouldn't have been the first time a girl, to be polite, had agreed to do something with me and not shown up.

Zach, waiting behind me, tapped me on the shoulder. Spaced out as I stood at the counter, Sarah, the girl waiting to take my order, looked at me as if I was weird. Which might have been true in a sense, I guess, but I still felt stupid. I ordered a small ham & pineapple pizza, paid, and looked for Lizzie.

"You seem a little distracted." Lizzie observed.

"Huh? No, I'm fine. I'm just a bit distracted," I responded.

She laughed at me.

"Something on your mind?"

"It's nothing."

Zach joined us and the conversation shifted away from me. The two started discussing some PlayStation game. I tried to be interested, I really did. But they were talking about some game I didn't have and I couldn't follow their conversation even if I'd wanted to. They were gushing over it, and while they made some vague attempts to keep me included, it wasn't working.

Pizza came to my rescue. Some people consider ham and pineapple an abomination but I am willing to defend my choice to the death. I ended up scoffing it down in some fit of twisted logic whereby my brain argued that the faster I finished the pizza, the sooner I could be at home, waiting for her to arrive. It was terrible logic, I knew it, and I did it anyway. I tried my best to hide my nervous excitement. They knew something was up, I could tell, but I think I got away with hiding my excitement enough not to come across any crazier than typical. Zach, the bastard, made a show of eating his pizza as slowly as possible.

"Sam, I know you're really into dinosaurs and all, but you can't be that excited about seeing this movie?" Zach said as we walked out of Corner Pizzeria. "How many times have you already seen these?"

I shrugged, noncommittal.

"I'm excited about dinosaurs, you know?"

That wasn't a lie; it just wasn't the whole truth.

"No, no I don't."

Tuesday Night December 9th 1997

We made it to my home at two minutes to seven. I gave a quick hello pat to Sorcha, my adolescent, misbehaving but ever-loving border collie, and rushed inside. I don't know what I was expecting.

My parent's house was a two-storey, dilapidated set of flats that they were in the process of renovating into a single house. They'd converted the two upstairs units into a single floor, which they lived in, while leaving me free reign over the downstairs unit.

My place was a popular venue with my friends and me as, some time ago, Dad had purchased a projector – 'because it was cheap' – without considering that they had nowhere upstairs to put it. I thereafter inherited an awesome set up for watching movies and we often took advantage.

The downstairs unit was in a constant state of renovation, as in, it currently looked like somebody had taken to it with a sledgehammer. Probably because somebody had actually taken to it with a sledgehammer. The main wall that divided what had previously been the kitchen and dining areas from the lounge room was an empty frame, complete with free hanging electrical wiring. The floor was bare concrete. Where the old downstairs entrance used to be, beside the prior dining room, they'd recently built a new internal staircase, unfinished of course, but at least saved the annoyance of having to go outside to get upstairs.

I'd set up the projector in the lounge room. To fill the room, Mum and Dad had given me an old couch, covered in bright red but well-worn cloth, that regardless of its cheapness and wear I found was amazing to sit on, and an armchair, leather and expensive but which I found terrible to sit on. Lizzie, disagreeing with my opinion, always claimed the armchair, while Zach preferred lying in front of the couch on beanbags, which left me with the couch to myself. Lizzie had gone upstairs 'on a quest to procure popcorn'. Those were her words, by the way. Zach tried restarting the conversation with me about the PlayStation game – the one with the name that I still can't remember. The conversation quickly became one-sided as he kept trying to explain it to me and while I pretended to listen, in reality I gave all my attention to my watch and the watching of seconds hand. I'm pretty sure he could tell I wasn't paying attention but he persisted anyway.

Seven twelve. Lizzie returned, her quest successful, and the smell of microwaved popcorn wafted throughout the room. Zach jumped up and tried to grab the bowl from Lizzie. She laughed as she frustrated his efforts, holding it away and turning her back to him as he tried everything to grab a handful. I, however, couldn't get myself interested in it. And I normally loved freshly cooked popcorn. And it's not like it was different to any other popcorn, which is to say, it smelt amazing. Any other day I'd be there with Zach trying to sneak a handful. Tonight, I couldn't bring myself to be interested.

While they were stuffing their faces with popcorn, I struggled to get the projector working.

"I don't know why you always have so much trouble with that projector," Zach said through a mouth full of popcorn. "For such a nerd, you seem to have a lot of trouble with basic technology."

Well, I thought, I was having a lot of trouble focusing. He had it sorted within moments.

By seven thirteen there was nothing left to delay proceedings. I curled up on the couch, somewhat disappointed and pressed play on the VCR remote. And I pressed it again because, like all remotes, it never worked the first time.

"Why do they always have these stupid anti-piracy ads?" Lizzie complained. "What's the point of putting them on the legit tapes?"

"Didn't you know? Everyone is a criminal these days," Zach replied.

"It's stupid that they make it so long that even if you fast forward it you still have to watch the whole thing."

The movie finally started. We cranked the volume. The squeals of a velociraptor set Sorcha barking, upstairs. I settled back as the first scene kicked in. Annoyingly, Sorcha was going crazy. Kind of like the velociraptor on screen. Zach rooted loudly for the raptor, cheering as it ate the first park worker.

"Shoot her! Shoot her!" Kate called out in perfect time with the character on the screen. Her head poked around the corner, a mix of curious grin and nervous smile.

I was stunned, shocked, frozen. Pick any appropriate adjective. My heart thumped away in my throat. I fumbled with the remote, trying to find the pause button.

"Could you not hear Sorcha going off?" Mum shouted as she followed Kate into the room. "Poor Kate here was waiting outside the whole time. I'm sorry, Kate; Sam was rude leaving you out there."

"It's ok, I wasn't there long," Kate replied.

"Ah, sorry…" I stumbled out an apology as I struggled to pause the movie. "I thought it was the loud movie that was upsetting Sorcha."

"Speaking of which, does it need to be so loud? You'll annoy the neighbours," Mum said as she turned and walked away.

"We'll turn it down, Mrs Price," Zach yelled out at Mum as she walked back upstairs.

The others watched stunned and silent as Kate walked into the room. She wore a loose white shirt with a V-neck cut that revealed more of her figure underneath than I was ready to cope with. She stepped over Zach and sat down next to me on the couch. According to the advertising, the couch was supposed to be a three seater, but we all know those are always a complete lie. There was only room for two people, side by side. She still sat in the middle. She gave me a smile, but it seemed as nervous as mine. And it's not as if I knew what to do, I felt like a fish out of water. All the knowledge in the world can't prepare you for when a pretty girl sits down next to you. Zach shook his head in wonder.

"I'm sorry I'm late. I, ah, had some problems getting here."

"Oh? What happened?" I asked.

"Let's just say I'm not supposed to be here. Technically, I'm not supposed to have left the house," she said. "Dad found out that I'd been driving the car around and since he… well…" Her eyes dropped and she went quiet for a moment.

She leaned against me and tucked her legs up onto the couch. "Don't worry about it. It's been ages since I've watched this movie. I'm glad I didn't miss much."

"I'm happy you made it."

"Me too."

I pressed play and for the rest of the night didn't notice another moment of the movie. Each breath, each shift of her body, each time her skin brushed against mine; I noticed it all and nothing else. I was anxious, overwhelmed by her presence. And it made me worried. Why me, my brain screamed. What did I have to offer her? And I barely knew her, why was I suddenly so infatuated? So fast.

"Relax," she whispered into my ear as she brushed her cheek against my shoulder.

Which seemed easy for her to say. But she was right; I needed to relax, lest she notice the rather physical effect she was having on me.

Then she touched my arm as her warm breath caressed my neck. A warm ripple passed through me and I sighed involuntarily. The corner of her mouth curled slightly. In her eyes, I could see a thousand emotions; the same nervousness and fear I held. Yet, beneath the dance that played out in her eyes, there was a new happiness. Content. And I stopped worrying. There was something different about her. It was the effect she had on me. As if I didn't need to understand how we fit together. I didn't need to prove anything to her. It was enough to intuit her. Perhaps that sigh was me letting go of all the tension and logic holding me hostage. I snuggled in a little closer and enjoyed the rest of the movie. Another lesson learnt.

As soon as the movie finished Zach and Lizzie turned to look at us, almost synchronously, in a way that seemed quite freaky. They both sat there staring at us, neither willing to be the first to ask the obvious question.

"Out with it," Kate said.

Zach, ever the outspoken one, spoke first. "Why the hell are you here?"

"Because Sam asked me."

"Sam… asked you?"

She nodded, grinning at their confusion.

"Really?"

She laughed. "Really."

"And you came?" Zach teased.

"Hey!" I grumbled.

She laid an arm around my neck. "Jealous?"

"So next movie then?" Zach said.

She laughed, then pulled her arm off me and patted my shoulder before leaning in again. Which confused the hell out of me. What did that mean?

An hour into the movie I noticed she'd fallen asleep, her cheek pressed against my shoulder while her hair fell over her face. How long had she been like that, I wondered? It was mesmerising, watching her chest rise and fall softly. Side note, I feel the need to point out here that this wasn't an excuse to stare at her breasts. She was just sleeping innocence. Everything about her infatuated me and I still didn't know why.

An hour and a half into the movie I realised that the situation as she lay asleep on me might soon become an issue, as my bladder started to protest vehemently against my heart's desire to leave her undisturbed.

By two hours, the situation was getting serious. I feared that even the smallest shift to adjust would be the cause to wake her and it would have been the most perverse cruelty to drag her from her innocence. I silently begged the movie to finish so I didn't have to suffer longer.

"You know," she whispered so quietly I barely heard her, "you could ask me to move."

"You're awake?" I whispered back, surprised.

She yawned. "Somewhat. You are rather comfortable. But I felt I've tortured you enough." She grinned at me. "But I appreciate the thought."

I returned, relieved, and slipped back onto the couch next to her as the final moments of the movie played out. As I sat back, she slipped her hand down the back of my arm. Her fingertips slide against my palm until her fingers parted mine. The movie finished too soon.

Zach and Lizzie were quick to their feet. They looked down at us, unable to comprehend what was going on. They shared a look as they stumbled to find something to say.

"I guess we'll leave you two to it," Zach said.

"Tell your Mum thanks for the popcorn," Lizzie said as they tiptoed out the door.

It was as if they couldn't get out the door fast enough.

"I guess that means it's time for me to leave too," Kate said. "Come walk me out."

She stood up and her fingers slipped away. I walked silently behind her as we stepped outside. As you might imagine, I didn't want her to leave, but I couldn't explain why.

"Why?" I asked as we stood at my gate. The word 'me' never quite made it from my mouth.

Her eyes dropped. "I don't know yet," she said smiling, more to herself than me. She shrugged. "It's like, I barely know you but, you know how sometimes you meet certain people who are just, different. They see people differently. When they meet, it clicks. There's something about you, the way you look at me. I can't explain it yet. But I want to feel it more. I'll see you around."

And she walked off. I sat at the gate and watched her until she disappeared around the corner.

"When will I see you again?" I asked the empty air where she once was. When indeed. I was so stupid. I had no way of contacting her. I had no idea where she lived, what she did during the day, where she worked. I had nothing.

Sorcha brushed against me, forever offering love. A scratch behind the ears is all I felt up to offering her. I walked inside, somewhat despondent.

In bed, I laid awake staring at the ceiling. It offered me no advice.

Wednesday Morning December 10th 1997

Breakfast was awkward. Mum had a look about her, stalking me to ask questions that I wasn't ready to answer. I poured some cereal into the oversized salad bowl I used as my breakfast bowl as she watched me expectantly, as if I would come forth willingly with answers. In my head, I begged her not to ask. I hoped she would just let me slide past. I wasn't so lucky.

"Well?" she asked.

"Well what?" I knew what she meant.

"Well… tell me more about the new girl from last night."

"I'm not sure what to say."

"She's pretty."

I nodded.

"Are you dating?"

How do you explain, 'not dating but I'd like to but I'm infatuated with her even though we only just met and I know nothing about her and nothing I think

38

about her is logical but somehow it still makes sense to me even though it doesn't'. I panicked.

I shook my head. The hint of a sly smile crept onto Mum's lips, but she kept the thought to herself.

"Well then I'm glad to see that you've made a new friend. What are you up to today?" she asked.

"I haven't thought about it."

Which of course was a lie. I'd thought about it. However, since the plan involved heading back out to my hideaway, it wasn't as if Mum needed to know. I'd always found the less information given out the better. I'd also decided, having thought about it for a long time but not gone through with it, to take up sketching again. When I'd woken that morning, I'd decided it was long past time to stop making excuses and actually do it.

It seemed like the time to find some inspiration. I used to draw all the time as a kid, but it had dropped away as I grew older. And I had since been periodically telling myself to pick it up again. That morning felt like a good time to do things differently.

"Well, spend time cleaning up downstairs, will you?" she said as she walked out the kitchen to get ready for work.

"Ok Mum." Yeah, she didn't believe it either.

I discovered a clean pair of cargoes hidden under a pile of laundry in the corner of my bedroom. Serendipitously, an old sketchpad was under the same pile of clothes. It was a lucky development and it saved me from what I expected was going to turn into an especially long search. I'm possibly the least organised person around. I threw the sketchpad and some neglected looking pencils into my backpack along with my current book. On my way out, I picked some things off the floor downstairs and threw them into my room. I couldn't see what was so bad about things down here, but mothers, you know?

My bike seat was wet. You'd have thought I would have learnt by now not to leave my bike outside. Wiping it off with an old towel soon turned into a tug-of-war game with Sorcha. Eventually, I managed to get my bike outside my gate, while keeping Sorcha inside.

My first stop was the 7-11 to pick up some Jolt Cola. So what if it was in the opposite direction? Nothing useful ever gets done without caffeine. It was a ten minute trip, but one I was well used to given that, a) I made it almost every day and b) the 7-11 was next door to the Corner Pizzeria.

I dropped my bike outside the 7-11 and headed to the rear of the store, where the cold drinks were kept. I took two bottles of the gods' divine cola-flavoured nectar and turned to the counter. I faced a girl, her back to me, with hair as vivid brunette as Kate's. It had to be her. I raced to catch her and my heart raced faster. I reached out to grab her shoulder. As she turned to walk away, I saw her face.

The girl looked nothing like her. Not even close. What the hell was I thinking? It would have been awkward. Well, more awkward. The cashier looked at me like I was weird. I paid and got out of there as quickly as possible.

As the path through the forest was decidedly bike unfriendly, I would always lock my bike to a fence near the entrance and walk the rest of the way to my retreat. That morning I headed straight for a big willow to sit under, pulled out my sketchpad and started to draw.

Started to, is still a bit of a stretch. An hour later, the paper was still blank. And I was frustrated because I used to draw all the time as a kid. Why did I have such a problem starting? Because all you drew as a kid were dinosaurs, I told myself. Well, maybe not everything, but at least half were dinosaurs. And if not dinosaurs, then birds. That's all I'd wanted to draw. And I was good too. Not amazing, but good enough. And having seen something once, I had no problem drawing it again from memory. No longer, it seemed.

I started scribbling, trying anything that came to mind. I tried drawing the forest, the falls and the trees, around me. The result was terrible; whatever talent I may have had as a kid, had clearly slipped away over the years. After a couple of sheets of sketch paper, which weren't cheap for a school kid with the lowest paying of jobs, and it still didn't look remotely like what I saw around me. Instead of the gratification I used to find drawing, all I found under that tree was frustration.

A noise startled me from behind, the loud rustle of leaves and a branch cracking. I turned, expecting to see her.

Caw! A flap of black wings and the crow disappeared.

Kate, what had you done to me? Why couldn't I stop thinking about you? I had started to become obsessive. And the worse thing about it all was the uncertainty.

Promising to myself that I'd come back to drawing, I put down the pad and pulled out the book I'd packed. I gave it fifteen minutes before giving up on that too. Some days just aren't good for focused activities. And I still had a few hours to burn before work.

I took my time walking back, anything to waste time and put off the rest of the day. On my return to the park, however, things got complicated. The fence to which I'd locked my bike was still there. My bike, my sole method of transport, however, wasn't. All that remained was a broken combination lock still wrapped around the pole. Those stupid bloody things were always shit. I kicked the pole in frustration, hard enough to hurt myself. So not very hard. Having my bike stolen complicated my life way more than I needed. It was a long walk home.

It was an even longer walk to work later that afternoon. I walked into Corner Pizzeria ten minutes late and set up at my food preparation bench in the backroom, hoping nobody would notice my late entry. The boss was a bastard when it came to lateness.

Lizzie ducked her head into the room.

"What happened to your bike?"

"Some bastard stole it."

"Really? Shit huh. That sucks."

"Lizzie! Counter!" the boss yelled out.

"Shit, I'll speak to you later."

She disappeared. Since I couldn't drive, and my boss still thought this was the sixties and only girls should serve customers, my main job was prepping food and cleaning up at the end of the night.

As if in punishment for my lateness, there was a large tray of capsicum waiting for prep on my bench.

Perhaps I hadn't gotten away with being late. I hate capsicum, so much and the bastard knows it. While I hate a lot of the so-called 'food' that ends up on top of most pizzas – which probably seems strange, given I'm willing to work with it – capsicum is number one on the list of foods I hate. I don't know who invented capsicum, but I wish them an eternity in hell. Just the smell had me dry retching. There were at least ten minutes worth of capsicum in that tray. I psyched myself up and started cutting. I made it eight before I needed to rush out the backdoor. A new personal best.

Once I'd composed myself enough to try again, I found Lizzie at the bench, the capsicum almost completed. She was laughing at me.

"I don't get it, it's only capsicum."

"Only capsicum? I don't get how anybody could enjoy those vile things."

She pointed to a tray of onions with her knife. "Get started on those at least?"

"You sure you want to be in here when I start those?"

"Somebody has to do this capsicum, are you going to finish them?"

I chose the onions and kept my mouth shut. Onions are third – maybe second, depending on my mood - on my list of food I cannot stand. What that meant practically was I could stand cutting them up, but woe be the person who puts them on my food.

"How are you and Zach going?" I asked.

"Oh, you know us," she sniffled, "… oh, those goddamn onions, why did I tell you to start cutting those."

She looked at me with red eyes and tears forming.

"What? It's the onions… really. It's just; sometimes he gets a bit much for me. You know how he is. We'll be fine."

By that stage, we were both in tears. It was getting messy.

"What about you? Tell me more about you and Kate," she said.

"There's not much to tell."

"No need to cry about it," she laughed. "But seriously, what do you mean there's not much to tell?"

"I mean, there's not much to tell."

"Bullshit. She randomly decided to come over and snuggle up last night for shits and giggles?"

"You saw that?"

"No, you were completely invisible and all I could see was the couch behind you, you idiot."

Which begged the question, how to tell her without telling her?

"We met up yesterday, we got talking and I invited her over. That's all there is to it."

"That's complete and utter bullshit. You expect me to believe that?"

"Lizzie! Counter!" our boss yelled.

Saved by the boss.

"We're not done discussing this," Lizzie said as she raced out of the room.

And I knew she meant that. Thankfully, she'd at least finished the capsicum; all I had to do was scrape it into containers.

I was elbows-deep in dishwashing water when Lizzie returned.

"When will you see her again?" she asked.

"I don't know."

"You don't know?"

"I maybe don't have any way of contacting her. I don't have her number. I don't know where she lives. You know?"

I shrugged.

"Oh, you idiot. You sweet, innocent idiot."

She shook her head and wandered back to the front of the store.

Lizzie chose to walk home with me after work. That wasn't unusual, her house was around the corner from mine, but I thought it silly that she walked her bike instead of riding ahead. We walked in silence for a while. Which was unusual. I was a little slow working out what was going on. Which wasn't unusual. It took me a while, but I eventually hinted onto the fact that she had something on her mind.

"You sure you're ok?" I ended up asking. "You seem a little distant."

"Huh? Yeah, I'm fine."

Which did nothing to convince me.

"I am, really," she added, perhaps sensing I didn't believe her. "To be honest, I'm trying to work out the best way to ask you about Kate."

"Oh?"

"So spill, tell me what happened."

"I can't."

She raised an eyebrow to that.

"Ok fine." She thought for a moment, "What is it that you like about her, then?"

Which led me straight to the question I'd been struggling with all day. However, I wasn't particularly good when it came to understanding my inner self. Or revealing it. It wasn't that I felt particularly private about anything. It was more because I was terrible at converting internal feelings into meaningful words. Every time I tried, it'd always come out as a jumbled mess.

"Everything," I said, taking a moment too long to respond.

Timing is everything when it comes to lying and being convincing. She rolled her eyes at me.

"To be honest, I don't know. It just happened. I barely know her. I don't understand what it is about her that I like. I just do. I can't explain it."

"Nawww, that's so cute."

"Gee thanks," I responded, unimpressed.

"Sam's got a girlfriend."

"We're not like that."

"Do you want to be?"

"I guess."

"You want to do more than just guess about those sorts of things Sam."

We stopped walking while I thought about it. She was right, of course. What did I want? I guess I wanted to see what would happen.

"How about I ask around and see what I can do about getting in contact with her for you?"

"Thanks."

She nodded and started walking again. I went to follow her.

"Sam," she said, looking at me concerned.

"Yes?"

"This is your house."

We were indeed standing in front of my house. I hadn't been paying attention to where we were walking.

"Shit."

"Bye Sam."

She was shaking her head as she walked away.

As I lay in bed that night, I kept thinking about Lizzie's question. What did I want? Every thought led to one answer. Her. I wanted her touch. I wanted her lips. I wanted her around me. I wanted more. I was hopeless.

Friday Afternoon December 12th 1997

Some unknown time before five and I'd spent the afternoon on my couch in my boxers and a dodgy old shirt, playing GoldenEye on my 64 and otherwise moping about. I didn't have work that night and Mother was in a particularly bad mood at me for not cleaning up enough. I'd turned the volume up to drown out the noise of her stomping around upstairs. It had been three torturous days since I last saw her and I'd concluded by that stage that Tuesday must have been some twisted dream. Not that I remember ever dreaming that vividly before, but I guess every now and then a dream will come along and completely blow you away.

Yeah, ok, I didn't actually believe that, but ultimately, I had given up seeing her again. It felt like I had been dumped. Which was a massive overstatement of the situation but that's still what it felt like. Well, as far as I suspected being dumped would feel like, given that I had no experience in the matter. Which was ridiculous. I barely knew her. It twisted me up inside. There was anger too. Anger at her for making me feel this way. Which was especially stupid, as if it was her fault. I was angry with myself for once again overthinking things, knowing damn well that I was doing it and still too stupid to stop myself.

"That isn't the look I had in mind for tonight. You're going to have to find something a little nicer to wear."

Kate stood in the dining room looking at me. She wore a stunning black dress that hung off her shoulders and hung loosely to her knees. The afternoon sun reflected a tiny hint of iridescence across her shoulder. A black lace choker wrapped around her neck. She looked amazingly beautiful. While her hair was tied back as always, tonight it was curled up into a bun while long sweeping bangs framed her lightly made up face with soft, shadowed eyes. With her head tilted and a curled-up half-smile on her lips, she took in my confusion.

"What are you doing here?" I asked. So I had been moping about not seeing her for three days and now, as she stood there, my first reaction was to question why? I was stupid.

"You're taking me on a date," she said.

"I am?"

She nodded once, her smile growing larger. My face grew redder.

"Yep, you're taking me to the movies."

"I am?" I said, my confusion increasing.

"Yes, so you're going to have to find something a little closer to my liking than what you currently have on."

"Shit."

I jumped off the couch and my mind immediately ground to a halt as it struggled to catch up with what was going on.

"Maybe you should start with a shower," she advised.

"Ah, yeah, that would probably be good a good idea."

That meant leaving her out there, though. I looked at her questioningly, uncertain what to do.

"Go. Have a shower. I'll entertain myself."

I'm not one to have a quick shower. I enjoy hot water far too much. I think I took twice as long in that shower as I washed everything in triplicate. I doubt a teenaged boy had ever been so clean.

It only occurred to me that I had no clean clothes in the bathroom as I went to dry myself off. That meant the risky proposition of wearing only a towel in front of her. And I knew that would become awkward. I considered putting the dirty clothes back on. Would that look bad though, I asked myself. Then again, which looks worse, dirty clothes or half-naked skinny boy?

I stepped out of the bathroom wearing only a towel. She sat on the couch, controller in hand. She wolf whistled in my direction. My cheeks turned a bright shade of crimson. As I walked past her to get to my room, she playfully tugged on the towel. Things almost got awkward. She laughed.

"Go! Put on some clothes already."

I pulled on a pair of black pants that were already hanging up ready for work, but all my 'good' shirts lay in the corner in a 'tidy' pile of unironed shirts. And they say boys don't care about what they wear. I picked up one of the better-looking ones. Rejected it. Picked up another and threw it away too. Rejected the third. I was running out of options. I'd never worried about this kind of stuff before? What kind of crazy magic was this girl casting on me? The last choice was simple, black. It was a wrinkled mess but it'd have to do.

"I'll be back in a moment." I said as I walked past her.

"No probs," she replied as she swung her head back and forth to see the TV better. "Just… hop out of the way of the TV, will you? I can't see anything past the glare of the sun reflecting off your pasty white body."

I walked upstairs in search of an iron. Mum must have heard, because she stuck her head out of the kitchen as I turned the corner. She gave me a look of mock disgust.

"Whoa, put a shirt on will you!" she joked. "We don't need to see that."

"Oh, don't you start as well."

"Oh is that so? I thought I had heard somebody else downstairs. Does somebody have a date tonight?"

I ducked into the study, hoping to find the ironing board in there, though if I'm being honest it was mostly to avoid answering her question. I felt a little more comfortable once I'd ironed the shirt and put it on.

"Well?" Mum asked as I tried to slip back downstairs again.

I got the feeling she already knew the answer and was simply teasing.

"Yes Mum. We're going on a date."

"Well, have fun then. Say hello to Kate for me."

Which wasn't the response I expected. Kate was still playing on the 64 once I got downstairs.

"Well, I was going to suggest we stay here and play games until we needed to be at the movies, but since you took so long in the shower and the movie starts at half six, I think we should head straight there," Kate said.

"Sorry."

54

"Don't be, you look smashing."

"Smashing?"

"Oh definitely, smashing. Now, shall we?"

I smiled as she took my arm and we walked outside.

"Wait, shit. I forgot. I don't have my bike."

I knew it was a stupid thing to say as soon as I'd said it.

"Wait, I'm guessing you didn't ride in that dress."

She shook her head.

"I can get Mum to drive us if you'd like?"

"Silly, I have the car."

"Oh, I thought there were issues last time?"

"Well, hopefully Dad doesn't notice it's gone."

"I can't believe you have your licence already."

"Who said I did?"

"Oh."

"If it helps, I'm going for my P's in a week."

"And your father lets you drive anyway?"

She gave me a funny look before speeding ahead of me, opening the passenger door for me.

"Isn't that supposed to be something I do?"

"This is the '90s Sam, and not the 1890s. Actually, it's just that there's a trick to getting the door open. You need to jiggle the handle correctly to get the damn thing open."

I slid into the passenger seat and she shut the door behind me. She jumped into the driver's seat, started the car and floored it, tyres screeching as we flew away from my house. I frantically scrambled for my seatbelt. She drove the whole way to the movies like a maniac, throwing the car around corners at what I thought were impossible speeds. I was beginning to see why her father might not like her driving. That is, ignoring the part where she didn't actually have her licence. I suppose that part was important.

"Aren't you worried about standing out to the police a little too much, driving like that?" I said, gripping the door armrest tightly.

"Are you saying I'm a bad driver?"

"I'm saying that maybe some people might... Yes. Yes I am."

She laughed.

"Are you afraid of dying Sam?"

"Right now, I'm more afraid of not making it to the end of the night with you."

She stroked my hand. "Cute."

Pulling into the car park for the movies, she headed immediate toward the rear of the parking lot, parking diagonally across two parking spaces.

"What?" she challenged. "Are you going to tell me I'm a bad parker now?"

I shook my head and hid my grin as best I could. I knew better than to answer that.

"So what are we seeing?" I asked.

"What's the one with DiCaprio and Kate Winslet?"

"Titanic?" I said, mortified that she was going to make me sit through that.

"Hah! Your face is priceless. Yes, that one."

She wrapped one arm behind me and one across my chest. Possibly to stop me from running away.

"Hey, imagine the points you'll score with me if you survive the whole movie."

Certainly a compelling argument, but for 'Titanic'. Was it worth it?

Once inside, she pointed toward the candy bar.

"Go get some popcorn, and I'll get the tickets."

"But…"

"Don't make me slap you Sam. Its 1997 remember, and don't forget, I dragged you out here."

"To be fair, I came willingly. Ok, but I'm paying for the next movie."

"That is, assuming we go on a second date," she teased.

"Oh."

She poked me and laughed.

"You are too easy," she said, pushing me toward the popcorn.

"Where do you want to sit?" I asked as we filed into the theatre.

"Quick, up the back."

There was a massive crowd of people trying to file into the cinema. We pushed our way through the crowd and took two seats in the middle of the back row of the theatre. The rest of the theatre filled up quickly. A rather polite woman sat next to Kate while I got some old guy who promptly hogged the arm rest whose subtle unpleasant smell soon got on my nerves. I leaned closer to Kate in an attempt to get away from him but she took that to mean that I wanted to get closer to her and tucked her head into my shoulder, an unexpected though pleasant outcome. And her hair smelt nice as it fell under my nose.

Her fingertips held my palm as her thumb stroked the back of my hand.

"I want you to draw me like one of your French girls," Kate whispered into my ear as a naked Kate Winslet lay down on the movie screen.

She giggled as I turned bright red.

"Stop teasing. Besides, I don't do life drawing."

"Oh, he finally fights back."

Her other hand joined the first.

"But you do draw?"

"A little."

"Interesting."

She laid her head back on my shoulder.

"Ok, that movie went for ages," she said, as the credits rolled and we shuffled out with the crowd.

Things hurt from sitting in that uncomfortable seat for the entire movie. But despite the rumours going around about the movie, frankly, it wasn't as bad as I thought it was going to be. It wasn't just a matter of surviving until the end; you might even say I enjoyed it. Sure, I cared a lot more about Kate's touch than the movie, but I hadn't found the movie completely terrible either. If that were the worst that I'd have to suffer to have her close, I'd suffer gladly.

"So here's what I didn't understand. Why didn't Jack get up on the door with Rose at the end?" she asked as we neared her car.

"Maybe because it kept trying to tip over when he tried to get on. Or maybe if he'd gotten on, with his extra weight it would have floated under the surface and they both would have frozen anyway, even if they were floating."

She pondered it for a moment.

"That actually makes sense," she said.

"Or, maybe it wouldn't have been so cloyingly sweet without the Hollywood ending? Insert generic heroic sacrifice and all that?"

"Smart arse. Hey, do you know what time is it?"

My watch said 10:12pm.

"This might seem like a silly question, but are you hungry?"

My stomach growled loudly in response. It wasn't until her mention of food that I noticed how hungry I was, being otherwise distracted before.

"Hah, me too. Were I smarter, I would have taken us to dinner beforehand. What are the chances of finding a place to get food at this hour?"

"That depends on how appalling the food is that you're willing to accept. Larry's Kebab Shop stays open until past midnight, but calling what he sells food is a stretch. It doesn't go into the deep fryer as food and it sure as hell doesn't come out resembling anything edible. I highly recommend sticking to the hot chips."

"Noted. That gives me an idea. Do you think you'd be interested in spending more time with me tonight?"

"Trick question?"

"I suppose it probably was."

Friday Night December 12ᵗʰ 1997

After our quick detour to Larry's and with an overly warm box of chips sitting in my lap, Kate drove east through the middle of town until we hit Sussex Beach. She pulled the car into one of the parking spaces that overlooked the beach and turned the engine off.

"I've got something I want to show you. Come on," she said.

Sussex Beach is a sheltered beach on the edge of town, roughly a kilometre long and saddled between small rocky ridges to the north and south. Picnic huts stand evenly spaced along its length beside a bike path laid parallel to the water's edge. It had been a long time since I'd been down there, and at night, even longer. The night solicited enchantment, the moonlight rippling over the black sea. I had no idea where she was taking me.

In her excitement, she left me behind, almost bouncing as she strode on ahead, leading me north toward the ridgeline.

"Come on!" Kate called, waving me on once she realised I hadn't kept up.

I had to run to catch up with her. She led me to a hidden path cut roughly across the rocky hillside, leading up over the ridge. I'd been to this beach plenty of times and I'd never noticed the path before. Showing some esoteric knowledge, she took my hand and led me up the dark path, avoiding all the cracks and unstable rocks and, at least for her, effortlessly climbed to the top.

As we topped the ridge, I saw that the path continued down the other side, twisting sharply around volcanic projections down the slope to a diminutive cove. Cliffs encircled a tiny beach not ten metres long and less wide. Years of tides had eroded away the base of the cliffs such that it looked as if the cliffs hung over the beach. On the far side of the small cove, the cliffs from the north and south converged until there was only a small gap for the ocean to enter. From the little beach, you could see the sky only by looking directly up. But the near full moon directly above us flooded the night with light. It was amazingly beautiful. That it had been here this whole time and I'd never known blew my mind.

Kate sat down on the sand, right at the edge of the water, tucked her knees up to her chin, and motioned for me to sit next to her. She pursed her lips and said nothing as she waited for me to sit down. The sand was slightly damp.

"You know how you have your special place? Welcome to mine. This is where I like to come when I need to get away from things. There've been times I've even spent the whole night here."

"I can see why you'd want to spend time here. This place is amazing. Like… wow amazing. It makes my place look boring."

"That's not true."

I shrugged. In my mind, the score was clearly Kate - 1, Sam - 0 when it came to special places to get away.

We opened the chips between us and I took the first one. It was worse than expected. How anything could fail to meet such low expectations as one may give to plain hot chips I have no idea but somehow these managed. Congratulations to the local fast food joints. We ate them all in silence. The air was crisp, and the soggy hot chips were soon soggy cold chips. It seemed so inconsequential to consider such a fault in the night's events that I laughed. The night was already beyond expectations. Those horrible chips merely highlighted how perfect everything else was.

"How often do you come out here?" I asked.

She thought about it for a while, staring out into the black waves.

"Often enough."

I didn't push. Where we hid our secrets was one thing; what sent us there, something else entirely. I took off my shoes, threw them behind me and stretched my feet into the water. The freezing water quickly soaked the bottom of my pants. I laid back on the sand and stared up at the stars.

"Aren't you afraid that we barely know each other?"

"Are you afraid of the stars?" she replied as she followed my lead and, lying back, threw her shoes behind her.

"No, why would I be?"

"Exactly. They just are. But the more you look up at them, the more you realise how much more there is to find."

She shuffled closer and laid her head on my chest. It took a moment to realise she was describing me. She had weaved the compliment so deftly that she left me stunned.

"Do you understand now?" she asked.

If I'd given a response, I would have said yes. But that would be like saying I knew how many grains of sand there were under my feet. I still had a long way to go before I'd fully understand.

"The water passed through his shoes and the stars through his soul," I quoted.

"Well, well, *Les Mis*, aren't you the romantic? How apt. Although I would like to point out that you tossed your shoes away quite a while ago."

"Actually, they made us study it in school this year. I hated it."

"I know. Me too."

We laughed.

"Why do you think they make us study books like that?"

"To make us more learned, of course." She rolled her eyes and scoffed once. "Do you want to know what I think? I think they understand that we teenagers are all searching for meaning in our empty lives, and they grasp desperately toward misguided attempts to guide us based on rote lessons of old, which are inevitably misaimed. I mean, I think reading and finding meaning within stories is important and shit, and it's a good thing that they try to push that on us, but different people will be different, you know? We all search for our own meaning. They focus too much on the rote others have come up with and not enough on the quest we need to travel to find out ourselves."

"Ok, so why don't they teach us more philosophy then?"

"Maybe because stories are like applied philosophy and since the philosophy has already been worked out for them they don't have to think about it.

"And the last thing we need is more nihilist teenagers."

She laughed.

"Fair point. We all go through that stage though. But there are too many stars to give up on them all."

"And some are brighter than others."

She pointed upwards.

"Is it cheesy to point out the shooting stars in a moment like this?"

"Definitely."

"Hah. Look, another," she said as one streaked across the sky.

"Question, why do we wish upon shooting stars? All they are is fireballs hurtling toward their inevitable doom, fated to burn out far too quickly. I'd rather wish upon the eternal beauty of the stars."

Her face appeared above me. "Sam, you continue to amaze me."

"I don't think I'm that amazing."

"I happen to disagree."

"What would you wish for?" I asked, trying to get away from talking about me.

She thought about it for a moment. And then she leant down. And I, in my naivety, didn't notice what was happening. That isn't to say that I purposely moved away. I flinched. In my defence, it was a new experience for me. But how best to describe what happened? She missed. Internally, I was screaming at myself. I quickly realised how much I'd screwed up. How could I be so stupid? I am lucky she recognised my reaction for what it was.

She didn't miss the second time. I still wasn't prepared. It was the lightest peck on my lips, her bottom lip barely brushing mine.

"I wish for chaos and dancing stars."

"I…I…I…" I stuttered as my mind melted down.

She laughed and laid her head back on my chest. Things suddenly became a lot more comfortable. Like her kiss shattered a boundary. We went from philosophy to kissing in under five minutes. I really liked this girl.

"What do you think draws teenagers to Nietzsche?" I asked.

"We're all searching for meaning, purpose, whatever. What do you think the meaning of life is?"

"Do you always ask tough questions like that? I'm not sure I'm ready for that kind of question this early in our relationship," I joked.

"Relationship? Who said anything about relationship?" She said flatly. Her face twitched as she tried to contain a giggle. "Relationship, I like the sound of that."

"I do too. But to answer your question, I don't think there is a purpose to life. And I like it that way."

"Why?"

"Because without a defined purpose, we're free to make our own."

"Like we're a blank canvas free to draw our own picture?"

"Yeah, something like that."

"So tell me then; what do you like to draw?"

"Figuratively or for real?"

"How about for real? Enough philosophy for a while. If not life drawing, then what do you like to draw?"

"To be honest, I've only started drawing again recently. I used to draw all the time as a kid, but it's only recently that I've decided to pick it up again. I've definitely gone a bit rusty."

"What did you used to draw then?"

"As a kid?"

"Yeah."

"You'll laugh, but I used to be obsessed with dinosaurs as a kid, and I'd draw them all the time. I've never outgrown my love of dinosaurs."

"Hence Jurassic Park the other night."

"Pretty much."

"Would you like your own pet dinosaur?"

"Hah, yeah, it'd be cute to have a pet velociraptor."

"Cute? Those things weren't cute."

"Definitely cute. You know, they weren't anything like in the movies. They're like, a third of the size that the ones in Jurassic Park are. About the size of a turkey. And they probably didn't hunt in packs, and they definitely couldn't open doors."

"So it'd be like having a pet turkey… only with teeth?"

"That's one way of looking at it."

"That doesn't seem particularly cute to me. I think I'll stick to having a real bird as a pet."

"You have a pet bird?"

"No, Dad won't allow it. But I'd love to have one. Or more. I love birds."

"What kind would you get then? Like a budgie or something?"

"Ick, no. Budgies are boring. I'd like something that would sing to me, like a canary."

"But you can't do much with a canary?"

"I think birds are more for admiring. I like birds like you like dinosaurs."

"But you don't have sketch books full of drawings of birds like I do of dinosaurs."

"No, I have albums full of photos of them."

"Oh?"

"You draw, I take photos. It's a hobby of mine. I like photographing birds. I admire the freedom birds have, the ability to fly wherever they want. They're so… majestic, I guess is the word I'm looking for. I like capturing that on film. It's as if, in each photo, I get to capture a moment of that freedom and make it my own."

"Wow."

"Wow?"

"It's that, Kate Rees, you are nothing like I would have expected you to be. And I guess I feel bad having thought otherwise of you."

By that stage, she had turned onto her stomach and had propped herself half on her elbows, half-lying across me.

"I never in a million years have expected to be lying on a beach discussing philosophy with a beautiful girl like you."

"And kissing?"

"Well, one kiss."

And then she kissed me again. Her bottom lip pressed firmly against mine, and stayed there forever. Or close enough, it's not as if I was counting.

"No, definitely kissing. What led you to those conclusions?" she asked.

"I guess with your group of friends, the cool group and all, I didn't think you'd be like that."

"Apology accepted. You're not the only person lying on this beach to have made the mistake of judging a book by its cover. And I think you'll find my friends are not so different once you get to know them."

"Assuming they're interested in meeting me."

"They will be. I'll convince them."

"Maybe."

"You'll survive," she said. "I think we should look at heading back though, the water's starting to get a little high."

I hadn't noticed, naturally. It was lapping around my thighs by that stage. My legs were freezing. I'd been completely oblivious.

"Shit, you must be freezing in that dress."

She shivered. "Now that you mentioned it. This dress wasn't the appropriate choice of attire for this little adventure."

We retrieved our shoes from the beach, though one of my socks never made it out, lost somewhere in the darkness, a sacrifice to the ocean gods for the amazing night perhaps. If that were the price for a night like that, they could have all my socks.

The path up to the ridge was slippery with dew and dark despite the moon. I quickly regretted not putting my shoes back on as we stumbled back to Sussex Beach. To add to this, it was freezing and we had begun shivering, making our climb treacherous.

The path transitioned near the top to an abrupt set of roughly cut concrete steps, each seemingly randomly spaced as they twisted the last few metres to the top. Kate misjudged the final step, tripping as the stairs flattened at the top. She landed hard on her knees.

"Are you ok?" I asked, helping her up.

She nodded, but it had clearly hurt. Still, she limped the rest of the way without complaint. It was only once we had reached the streetlights of the beach car park that I could see that her slip had grazed her knees badly.

"Are you ok?"

She looked at me, confused. I pointed to the blood trickling slowly down her left leg.

"Your knee?"

She turned to get a better look in under the street light.

"Fuck," she swore. "And my dress is ruined too. Don't worry, I'll be fine, I can barely feel it. I've had worse."

She stepped up to me, wrapped an arm around my waist, and looked me in the eyes. "It was totally worth it."

My hands came away covered in sand. She showed me hers, as covered.

"You know, you're completely covered in sand," she giggled.

"We both are."

We laughed.

"Hold still a moment," she said as she brushed off what sand she could. Then she spun and presented her back to me.

"My turn," she said cheerfully.

I started brushing the sand off the back of her dress. She jumped.

"Butt!"

"But?"

"No, butt! That's my butt you're touching."

"Oh shit!" I apologised profusely as I held my hands away. Had I screwed things up?

She laughed.

"I just didn't expect you to be so forward."

"I promise, it was an accident."

"Uh huh, of course it was," she said before poking her tongue out at me.

"Honest. Though…"

"That's going to take a few more dates, mister. Now let's get you home."

She slammed the brakes on and pulled the car to a screeching stop outside my house. I was a little reluctant to get out and bring an end to the night.

"When will I get to see you again?"

"Oh, I think I'll drop in unannounced as I feel like."

"Waiting for you this week almost killed me. I thought I'd never see you again."

"You thought that? That wasn't my intention, sorry. I can see how that might suck. I have work tomorrow, but how about Sunday, what are you doing then?"

"Nothing important."

She leant over and kissed me on the cheek.

"Then I'll be around some time on Sunday. Good night Sam, dream sweetly."

It was a long while before I slept that night.

Saturday Night December 13th 1997

Saturday was an anxious day, spent thinking about her and Sunday. The thought of her with me refused to stop floating. Work that afternoon was supposed to distract me. You can guess how well that worked.

"So… news about Kate?" Lizzie asked.

"Maybe."

She waited, expectantly.

"Well, spill?"

"She came around on Friday."

"And?

"And we went out on a date."

Her face lit up.

"And?"

"And it was nice."

"It was nice? Sam," she said, exasperated, "help me out here and cough up some details here."

I struggled internally with how much I was going to I tell her. I felt hesitant to tell her more than I understood myself.

"We went to the movies."

"And what did you see?"

"Titanic."

Her face twisted up.

"Your choice or hers?"

"Hers, I guess."

"Oh, she's evil, that one."

"Actually, honestly, I didn't mind it."

"Oh no! We're losing you to the dark side." She laughed. "It's cute though. Well done, she's beautiful. Oh and while I'm here, the boss is on the warpath. Casey broke some glasses and he's pissed. Keep your head down."

"Thanks for the warning."

"Lizzie!" The boss shouted.

"Oh shit."

She rolled her eyes and ducked out to the front again. I returned to scrubbing plates.

We walked home together again later that night.

"So, how about you and Zach?"

"There is no me and Zach. Not anymore."

"Oh."

She shrugged. It wasn't a shrug of uncertainty, more a shrug of 'I'm lying to hide my feelings'. She could keep her illusion though, my thoughts were more along the lines of – shit; here we go again. And I was stuck in the middle as both sides fought for my attention. Frustrating, because I always refused to pick sides between them, no matter how convincing they tried to be. Not that either of them had a convincing argument, either way. But it left me in the perilous position of potentially losing them both. Neither of their egos could take me sitting on the fence. So I prepped myself for a another period of dancing around their feelings and cajoling their egos until they settled back down, forgot about whatever caused this breakup and we started the cycle again. The worst part was, frankly, that they were damn near perfect for each other. And they knew it too. They just hadn't learnt how to solve their problems. So more than anything, I prepped myself to be the balance between them expecting the world settled again and order to reassert itself. Until then, though, I danced to their needs.

"What happened?"

She shrugged again. I held my poker face, I knew that I just had to wait it out and she'd be forthcoming, but I was silently begging her not to make me drag it out of her.

I know that that comes across the wrong way. I meant her no ill will. It was that I hated being stuck in between them. It was frustrating. I didn't know how to fix them. That is, I didn't know what I could tell them to help them break the cycle. The inevitable talk that I'd have with both of them would go the same way. We'd end up talking, separately of course, and then they'd thank me for all the help I'd been. Without me actually doing anything. And it's not as if I was telling them anything they didn't already know. Hell, most of the time, I was there to give them somebody who would nod and smile the right way while they solved their problems themselves. Still, I was, somehow, the relationship guru, as if I had a clue. I didn't get it, but I guess I was what they needed.

I shrugged and flashed her a questioning look, body language to tell her I couldn't help until she broached information first. I would describe what I saw on her face as her cracking, but that simply wouldn't be fair to her, to imagine it as some war between us. She was only fighting herself. She was protecting herself. Trying to work out if it was safe to open up and expose herself to me. No matter how well you know a person, we all experience that fear. I couldn't blame her for it. If anything, I was happy she would, I know I wouldn't be able to.

"We had a fight."

"About?"

"I don't think you want to know."

"Well, that's up to you."

She struggled to put the words together. I'd never seen her struggle as visibly as she was then. But it seemed clear by that point that she wasn't ready to talk and there was no point pushing her. I wrapped an arm around her shoulder to comfort her.

"Sex. It was about sex," she blurted out.

That was a new topic between them.

"Specifically, how he doesn't ever seem to want to have any with me anymore. He kept turning down, like what the fuck? I mean, what fucking guy doesn't want to have sex? Like, he doesn't want me anymore. I don't know. I could see it in his eyes. He wasn't interested in me anymore. We fought about it. It's just... just look at me though? It's little wonder. I'm hardly the most attractive girl around." She shook her head. "You don't have to listen to this."

That actually didn't seem like Zach at all. Certainly, not according to the way he would describe Lizzie to me. While he'd never mentioned sex before, still, he was always glowing in the way he described her, especially physically speaking. Often with a little too much detail. There had to be more to it, that doesn't seem like the reason at all. Now I'd have to ask him why, without asking why. That is, it meant I'd have to find out from him the reasons, without making it obvious to him that I'd spoken to her in case that would cause more problems. The dancers spun. But what was I to say to her?

"He hadn't told me anything."

"I know. You couldn't have done anything anyway. I'm just angry."

"Angry because you feel like you couldn't do anything?"

"Exactly. But enough about my sorry relationship, what about yours? It was obvious you weren't telling the whole truth when you said you guys went to the movies."

I swore silently. What was I supposed to say to her?

"Ah…" I stuttered.

I thought I'd dodged that question.

"It's still early days."

"Well I hope it turns out better than mine."

And with what was I supposed to reply to that? 'Yes, I hope so too?' I shrugged. The ever-faithful non-answer. By then, thankfully, we'd made it to my place and I could get away without saying anything further. I waved goodbye and walked inside.

Sunday Morning December 14th 1997

I washed, dressed and redressed myself. And they say us nerds don't care about what we wear. It's not true; we're just no good at it. Still, I had no idea what plans she had in mind for today, which made it hard to prepare.

I spent the rest of that morning on my couch, wasting the day away while I waited for Kate to appear. Lesson learnt, next date get an approximate timeframe for things to occur.

Not long before lunchtime, there was a burst of activity upstairs. I heard Mum talking to someone, though it was incomprehensible through the floor between us. The tapping of footsteps followed as somebody walked down the internal stairs. My excitement rose, like, real heart in throat kind of stuff. It was about time she came over. So I guess I shouldn't have been surprised at the weird look Zach gave me when I greeted him with a beaming smile as he walked around the corner. And then the look of massive disappointment that I'm sure followed.

"Geez, it's good to see you too," he said.

"Sorry, you weren't who I was expecting."

"It seems I never am who people expect me to be."

"What do you mean by that?"

"Lizzie and I broke up."

"So I heard."

"Oh." His voice dropped.

"What happened?"

"I didn't want to do it anymore. I don't know. It was like, I tried and I tried but I wasn't happy. And it was wearing at me and wearing at me. I finally decided that it wasn't going to change so I pulled the plug on Friday. Breaking up sucks, but I couldn't pretend like I was happy anymore."

"Fair enough."

"So I came around to grab you so we can catch up and you can help me forget things."

"I can't."

"What do you mean you can't?"

"I can't. Kate is coming around today."

He gave me a look to say he didn't believe me.

"Wait, take a step back. You said you already knew. Have you been talking to Lizzie? You're not taking her side are you?"

His voice kept rising.

"No." I said with a sigh and shake of my head.

It was clear he didn't believe me. This was typical them though, dragging me in between their two giant egos. The two of them could be so self-centred and frustrating at times. All this bullshit I did to avoid looking as if I'm favouring one over the other.

"No really, Kate's coming around soon."

He still didn't believe me.

"Seriously? You'd seriously pick a girl over a brother?"

He stormed off, marching straight past a confused Kate. He was so up himself, I doubt he even saw her. The moment ruined my excitement.

"What's his problem?" Kate asked.

"He and Lizzie broke up."

"Oh, in that case we can do this another time if he needs you?"

"He'll be fine. He just needs some time to get over himself."

"But why was he so upset with you?"

"We go through this every time those two break up. I get stuck in the middle of them as they both try and get me to pick a side."

"I'd say something about that not being at all like a good friend, but I know what you mean."

"It's ok, give them a few weeks to think about it, they'll get over it and get back together. They are repeat offenders. I'm sorry, I was excited about seeing you, but his little spat really dampened my mood."

"Well then let's get out of here and do something about that."

"What are we up to?"

It was difficult to tell what she had in mind. She wore simple, casual clothes; a plaid shirt with her sleeves rolled up, tight jeans over walking boots and a small backpack slung over her right shoulder.

"I'm taking you on a picnic. I thought we might do some bird watching and I brought my camera to take some photos. Which, now that I think about it, probably sounds somewhat boring for you. I'm terrible at this, coming up with things to do, thing."

Which was the opposite of what I thought. It sounded like something I'd actually enjoy.

"It sounds nice, actually."

She sat down next to me and curled up into me.

"Or we could stay here?" she said as her hand found mine.

"Tempting."

She jumped up quickly and pulled at my hand. "Come on, before we get too distracted."

"I think I would have liked distracted."

She wrapped an arm around my neck, pulled me closer until her lips were a fraction of an inch away from mine.

"I bet you would!" she whispered.

Then she pushed me away and walked off, leaving me hanging.

"Well, are you coming or not?"

She had the biggest grin. And I, a smitten puppy on her leash, followed her out the door. I gave the rather excited Sorcha a scratch as I closed the gate behind us. She had more experience acting like the excited puppy. I had much to learn.

"Morning Kate," Mum called out from the window above us.

"Hello Mrs. Price," she responded.

"Will you be home for dinner Sam?"

I wasn't sure what the answer to that was.

"He probably won't be Mrs. Price, but I promise you I won't keep him out too late."

Mum laughed. "Well, tell him he needs to invite you along for dinner sometime soon. And have fun."

We walked down my driveway, hand in hand. "Lunch and dinner?"

"I hadn't planned it, but stuff it; since I brought lunch, I figure you can take me out to dinner afterward," she said with a grin.

"Where's your car?"

She sighed. "No car. You don't mind walking?"

"Not at all. Where are we going?"

"I thought it'd be good to heading back to where we first met. It's a nice spot there."

We headed toward the park in silence. The longer we walked, the more awkward the silence between us grew. Mostly, I spent the time wondering if she was expecting me to start the conversation. But I didn't know where I was supposed to begin. And the more I struggled, the further I seemed to get from something to talk about.

"Something up?" she asked.

"I was thinking how terrible I am at small talk. I don't want to seem awkward."

"Relax. I'm the same. It's nice being able to share silence with somebody for once."

A rustle of leaves caught my attention. We'd set ourselves up in my favourite spot, with our feet in the creek, me with binoculars in hand, while she looked around hoping to catch something with her rather professional-looking SLR type camera. I held up the pair of binoculars that she had brought with her and I tried, in vain, to get the damn things to focus. All I saw was a splash of black in the fuzzy green. I was supposed to point out the birds for her so she could take photos. At this, I sucked. I pointed toward where I had seen the black splash.

"Was that something?"

She laughed.

"It was probably a raven."

"No good?"

"They're a little too common for an interesting photograph. A bit too plain and boring."

"I'm a little plain and boring."

"Don't get me wrong, I think they're beautiful and supremely intelligent, just not what I'm looking for at the moment."

"Oh."

"Oh, shit. That's not what I meant. You are beautiful and intelligent and exactly what I'm looking for. I was just hoping to spot something other than crows today."

"Ravens, you mean."

"Same diff."

"I always wondered what the difference is between a crow and a raven."

"The short answer is that it's complex, the long answer is that it's really fucking complex. The quick answer is that there isn't any real difference. It's not like all corvids decided one day to split with crows on one side and ravens on the other. It essentially comes down to whatever the person naming the species felt like at the time. Ravens tend to be the bigger than crows, but here in Australia it's even more complex."

"But the birds in this place are ravens?"

"Probably. Good old Aussie Ravens. They're the most common species around here."

"Well, maybe if I could work out these binoculars I could actually help you find something more interesting."

"Don't worry about it, I'm not."

She capped her camera and placed it back in her bag. Holding the bag, she shuffled close until I could feel her breath against my cheek.

"The birds can wait."

She kissed me, firmly, on my left check.

"I say we eat some of this food I brought and work out what's going wrong after? Now, I hope you're ok, but I don't have that much to spend on food," she said as she pulled out a bottle of wine, "especially after I forked out for this bottle of wine. It's not cheap to buy alcohol when you have to pay somebody else to buy it for you, especially when you don't have a lot of money in the first place. All I could get was cheese and these awesome-looking baked bread rolls."

"I can't believe you bought a bottle of wine. It sounds good."

"You can't have a picnic without wine, Sam. It's the rules. Though, don't expect a lot from this wine. I gave my supplier a ten and got change."

She took out two plastic cups, deftly opened the bottle, poured out a cup and handed it to me.

She poured another cup and handed it to me as well. "Hold please."

She pulled out two paper wrapped bread rolls.

"Swap," she said holding out one roll.

"Plastic cups, classy, I know." She shrugged.

As if I cared.

"It's not like I would have a clue when it comes to wine."

"Well, all you need to know is that pinot noir is the only way to drink red wine."

"Noted."

Her face screwed up as she took the first sip. "Ok, it's a bit of a stretch to call that wine, but it'll have to do."

As I said, I didn't have a clue when it came to wine and as with the vodka previously had with her, drinking that cup was a first for me. I struggled, though I did my best to hide my displeasure with it as much as possible. If this was what wine is, it did nothing for me. I think the vodka burnt less going down. I suffered through sips between bites of bread roll, which, on the other hand, was fresh and delicious."

"Yeah, I know, the wine is not much chop, but the alcohol helps us forget."

"Helps us forget?" I asked, curious as to what she meant.

"Oh, it's nothing. Our problems, I guess."

"It doesn't sound like nothing."

Pursed lips told me to let the issue slip.

"Another glass?"

As I tried to think of a polite way to say no, she had already half-filled it.

"Have you ever tried to climb to the top of that waterfall?" she asked.

I shook my head.

"Why not?"

"Because the rocks are wet and slippery and I didn't see the point."

"Because you're scared?"

"That too."

"Why?"

"It's a rocky cliff face."

"It's only a few metres high."

"More like ten."

"It doesn't look all that difficult. Come on Sam, not everything in life is going to have a point; you have to experience some things."

She put down the last uneaten bit of her roll, put her bag behind us and jumped up.

"You're not serious?" I asked.

"Of course I'm serious."

"What about the food and wine?"

"They will still be here when we get back. Come on, no excuses."

She slung her camera around her neck and trudged off toward the waterfall, pushing aside shrubs and branches as she went. She was right, I figured. Sometimes you needed to risk it. I had no idea why I hadn't bothered to climb the falls. Effort? I was actually excited about climbing it as I chased after her.

And then I reached the rock face and looked up. Fear. Regret. From that angle, I could see that while it wasn't exactly sheer, it was certainly more vertical than horizontal. She was already a few metres up. I hadn't gotten anywhere and I was already stuck. Looking down at me, she pointed to a large rock in front of me.

"Start there."

I worked my way slowly up the rock face, watching her closely and following her every step. Despite getting soaked from the water falling to my right, the rocks weren't as slippery as I thought they would be.

The truth is that getting to the top didn't end up being anywhere near as difficult as I had expected. There wasn't a whole lot of room up there. She'd placed herself closest to the running stream, which meant I had to climb over her to reach an open place to sit. The water trickled down beside us and over the edge. Our legs hung over the edge as we looked out into the tree canopy. She was glowing.

"See, easy."

"Yeah, ok, you were right."

"Told you so."

The view from the top was a completely different perspective on the place. More leaves and fewer tree trunks. It wasn't quite high enough to break through the canopy, but it was warmer and more sunlight bled through. Also, the ledge was completely covered in bird poop and what looked to be an abandoned bird nest in the form of a mess of grass and feathers tucked away from the edge.

Kate picked up a feather and twirled it in her fingertips.

"This is a good sign."

"What kind of bird is it from?"

"No idea, some kind of hawk or some other bird of prey I'm thinking."

She dropped the feather into the stream and we both watched as it quickly disappeared over the edge.

"Quick, give me the camera, quick!" She pointed excitedly into the trees. I couldn't understand what she could suddenly be so excited about. Hell, I could barely tell where she was pointing.

"It's around your neck."

"Oh, I knew that."

I passed her the camera and she started clicking off shots immediately.

"What is it?" I asked.

"Look."

"All I can see is a dark bird that looks a lot like another raven from here."

"It seems your raven isn't a raven at all. See — look at the white tips of its tail and wings."

"It still looks like a raven to me."

"Can you see its yellow eyes?"

She sounded so excited that I'm not sure she actually heard me.

"It still looks like a raven to me."

"It's called a pied currawong. It's kind of like a big black magpie. I mean, they're not that rare or anything, I've just never seen one before. It's neat for a bird nerd like me, just like it would be neat to find the owner of this nest."

"Ok, so do you have like an 'ultimate bird'? Is there one kind of bird that you'd love to photograph but haven't had the chance to yet?"

She smiled, more to herself than me.

"I'm not sure I'm ready to reveal that much of myself. That's a deep question."

"Really?"

"It is for someone like me. But, I think for you I'll answer it. I've always wanted to just sit and watch a lyrebird for days upon days. Photograph it? Sure. But I'd give anything just to see one. To watch it sing."

"A lyrebird is the bird that's on the 10 cent coin right? With the fancy tail?"

"That's the one."

"Are they rare? Why a lyrebird?"

"They're not that rare. And why? I guess it's because I sympathise with them. What's so amazing about the male lyrebirds – it's the males that do all the singing – is how uniquely capable they are of impersonating the songs of all the birds around them, and heaps of other sounds too. They're like singing chameleons, I guess. They're so good at it that they can even fool the birds that they're copying. But I've always wondered; do they have their own song? I mean, when everyone knows you are so good at copying everyone else, when you're so good at blending in, what happens when you sing your own song? Does anybody believe it's even yours? Does anybody notice? I want to hear a lyrebird sing his own song, not some other birds' song. I want to sit there and tell him he doesn't have to pretend anymore. That it's ok to sing his own song and listen and just acknowledge him."

It hurt that I had nothing to respond to that with. I'd never felt as inadequate as I did then. Each time we talked a little more of her apparent pain would slip out. What was she getting at? What could I do to help her? Nobody teaches you this stuff. Was I supposed to point out what I noticed and draw her feelings closer to the surface where she'll be reminded of it? Or was I supposed to sit there and listen and risk not doing enough? I think that's what made me feel inadequate, being frozen by indecision. Surely though,

94

doing nothing and hoping for the best was the worst option?

"I would listen to your song."

"That's why I like you Sam, there's something about you that lets me be me around you."

She smiled off into the distance, avoiding my gaze for the moment.

"It's beautiful up here."

I matched her gaze for a minute or so until the moment passed.

"It needs more wine though. Wait here. I'm going to go back and get it."

She slung her camera over her neck and then she was gone, over the edge and out of sight. The process of going over the edge looked difficult and somewhat awkward. It made me seriously wonder what I had managed to get myself into. Still, I twisted myself around on the ledge so that I could hang my head over the edge and watch her as she gracefully descended.

"Stop looking down my top!" she yelled up at me.

Until that moment, it had never occurred to me. Naturally, her comment had the opposite effect.

"I can't see anything!" I yelled back.

She reached the bottom. "Are you saying there's nothing there to see?" she said as she looked up at me.

That was one of those questions you come across in life where there is no right answer. And I'm sure she loved the look of panic I had on my face because of it. I guess so, because she poked her tongue out at me in response.

She jogged off toward her wine, and I soon lost sight of her as she disappeared into the trees between us. But she was quickly back again, almost skipping as she passed through the forest with her bag slung over her back. She made an exaggerated motion of adjusting her shirt once she reached the bottom of the rocks. But she was smiling, looking up at me as she started climbing up. She was quick up the cliff, jumping rapidly between rocks, casual and carefree. Too carefree.

Sunday Afternoon December 14th 1997

She was four metres off the ground when she slipped. Moments before, she'd be hanging with her left leg bent precariously high, as her right leg hung in balance. She'd reached upwards, ready to grab the next rock when, as she pushed off with her left leg, her left foot failed. Her left wrist fought vainly as her momentum twisted her body awkwardly away from the rocks. Her knees made a horrible scrapping noise as she swung her feet looking for purchase against the rock in front of her. I watched as fear spread across her face. Then her fingertips lost the battle against gravity. Her right hand clutched desperately at rocks in front of her. For a moment, her fingertips caught against the edge of a rock face. But they didn't hold. Her body twisted back the other way. She fell.

The scraping noise her clothes made as she slid down the rocks sounded horrible, but it was the sickening crunch as she hit the ground, left hand first, that was horrifying. She curled into a ball, her left hand held tightly as she rocked back and forth in obvious agony.

"Are you ok?" I yelled down at her.

It was a stupid question. Of course she wasn't. That much was obvious. It slipped out of me; a reflex response to the situation. Grimacing, she shook her head through the pain.

Heading back down was nerve-wracking. I would have had enough problems with it as it was, but having watched her fall made me so much more nervous. Another part of me told me I didn't have time for that; all I could think of is how much I had to get down to her. That first part was the worst, as I hung my legs off the edge of the cliff and blindly aimed for a foothold. My right foot eventually found purchase, but as soon as I went to put weight on it, it slipped. It was a tense moment as I hung on with all my strength. My heart raced, my fingers burned, and in that moment, all I could think of was joining her at the bottom far sooner than intended.

In the end, I made it down with only a slightly scraped knee. Reaching the bottom was a short-lived relief. I raced to her side.

"I think it's broken," she said.

There wasn't much doubt about that. Her left hand, red and swelling, hung awkwardly as she nursed her arm against her chest. Her eyes were rimmed red and her face was twisted in pain, but at least she could talk. I sat down beside her and wrapped an arm around her shoulders.

"Do you think you'll be right to walk? I'll take you home so you can go to a doctor."

She shook her head. "I can walk, but I don't want to go home."

"Well ok, but you need to go to a doctor. Why don't we walk to my place and Mum can drive us?"

She nodded. "Can you help me up?"

I tried my best to help her up gently but she still winced as she struggled to get back to her feet. As she stood upright, she cried out in pain as the body of her heavy camera swung around her neck and wacked into her hand. I grabbed it and went to lift it over her head, with all intention of carrying it myself. We both watched in horror as the lens fell away from the camera body. The fall must have bumped it. I reached out in vain, but my fingertips only served to push it further away. It hit the ground with a faint but audible crack.

"Oh no," she gasped. "No! No! No!"

I picked up the camera lens. As I held it up to the light, a massive scratch was clearly visible in the glass lens. She was breathing heavily, deeply upset. I handed the lens to her. She took one quick look at the lens, swore, and then angrily threw it at the ground. Then she grimaced in pain as her broken hand shifted.

"Are you ok?"

"Yeah." She said disheartened. "It's just, that's a $200 lens. It took me forever to save for it. I can't afford to replace it. And that's a cheap one. Photographing is my life. Now it's gone."

"Do you have a spare?"

"No." she responded angrily. "Fuck. Sorry, it's not your fault I'm angry, it's my own stupidity, and it's cost me, big time. I don't know what I'm going to do."

"Come on, there's nothing you can do about it now. Let's get you to a doctor. If you hold your wrist above your heart, it'll help."

She stormed off, clearly in pain and frustrated. I picked up the broken lens and shoved it in my pocket, then collected her bag and ran to catch up with her.

Mum quickly rushed us to the local hospital. Or at least what counted as the local hospital, a town our size couldn't support a real hospital. It was really a glorified doctor's surgery. It took a while to convince Mum that we would be ok and she didn't need to hang around. I had to promise I'd call her as soon as we were done. She still insisted on giving me some change for the payphone.

We waited two hours in that emergency room before a doctor finally saw Kate, which I thought was ridiculous. There were people seen before us that were obviously less urgent. Neither of us spoke much in the waiting room. We leaned against one another in the uncomfortable chairs and stared out as broken people filed in and fixed people filed out. Or was it that fixed people filed in and broken people left?

While she was with the doctor, I stole a pen and some paper from a nearby counter and wrote down the model number for her broken lens. I didn't have a clue when it came to cameras, or camera lens, but with Christmas coming up a plan formed in my head. I wasn't sure I could afford the $200 she said it was worth. But I figured there might at least be a cheaper option that I could find to get her started again.

Having never broken a bone before, or, for that matter, spent any time in a hospital, I had no idea how long she would take. I was quickly bored out of my mind. A side table offered only two options to do something about that – the Woman's Weekly magazine or the Cleo magazine. It was a tough choice. While I figured I could plausibly deny the Woman's Weekly magazine if caught, as insanity caused by extreme boredom, the Cleo, on the other hand, I was strangely curious about, especially given the article subjects shown on the cover. What teenage boy wasn't curious about what 'The hottest sex act ever – no bed required' could be? Curiosity won in the end.

I think I read every article I was so engrossed. Except the aforementioned article, that turned out to not be that educational. Nevertheless, I was so caught up in the article I didn't notice her standing over me, waiting patiently with her wrist newly cast.

"Whatcha reading?" she said, poking her head over the top of the magazine.

I turned bright red. Busted. Oh well, I figured the only thing to do was to run with it.

"I'm learning what it's like to sleep with hundreds of men."

She could barely contain her laughter.

"Is that something you're interested in taking up?"

She lost it when she saw my eyes widen in terror. But hey, at least she seemed happy again. I enjoyed seeing her face light up at my awkwardness.

"How does it feel?" I asked, pointing to her cast.

She lifted it up to show it off; its icy white made heavy contrast even to her pale skin.

"It's weird, really weird. And heavy. It's going to be interesting."

"Annoying?"

"We shall see. Being left handed is hard enough as it is, without having one of these to get in the way. I'm going to have to work out the mechanics of certain things. Some of the more important things in life are going to be a little difficult over the next few weeks, if you get my drift."

"I could see how that could make certain things difficult," I responded laughing. "Are you ready to go then? I'll call Mum to come pick us up."

"I guess so."

Talking on the pay phone in the lobby of this place surrounded by all these sick people felt weird. The place had hard vinyl floors and cold concrete walls and every sound echoed through the entire room. I hated talking on the phone at the best of times, but this felt invasive, as if these people should be privy to my private conversation. It felt like everyone was watching me. God I hate phones. I'm lucky it was a short conversation.

I was glad when she suggested that we wait outside the hospital; I needed to escape the sickness inside. A high brick wall fenced the entrance to the hospital car park and we climbed up it to watch the dusk slowly settle over the warm summer night. Which was more than a little stupid, come to think about it.

"I hope that not every day goes so horribly wrong like this one," she said.

"Today could have been worse."

"How so?"

"It could've been without you."

She responded by laying her head on my shoulder. My thoughts kept dragging me back to what she said earlier, about the lyrebirds. It weighed on me. It obviously signified something more than she let on. Ideas developed. I wondered if I had a way to fulfil that little life goal in some small way, and whether it would remain meaningful if I did. But how was I to broach it with her?

"Hey, what are you thinking about?" she asked.

"Oh, it's nothing."

"Bullshit."

Well, that was certainly true.

"Let's do it," I said.

"Let's do what? Bullshit? You are a strange person Sam Price."

"Have you ever been to the zoo?"

"I didn't know we had one."

"Well, I mean the one that's up north."

"Ok. But why the zoo? I mean, I'd love to, but why on earth were you thinking about the zoo?"

"Lyrebirds. I keep thinking about what you said. And I thought, they have a whole bunch of Australian birds there, surely they have a lyrebird section."

A long kiss followed her smile.

"Even if they don't, I would like to go there. I'd like that a lot."

Somebody coughed loudly. I jumped. Dad. How he'd managed to pull the car up to us without either of us noticing, I have no idea.

"I hate to interrupt, but your mother threatened to start cooking if we took too long and I'm scared to leave her alone in the kitchen for too long in case she burns the house down. You must know, Kate, while Sam's mother has many talents, cooking isn't one of them. Now, Sam, are you going to introduce me?"

"Umm, Kate this is my Dad, Dad, this is Kate," I said awkwardly.

"It's a pleasure to meet you Kate. Sam's mother has been gushing over this beautiful young girl that Sam has somehow managed to start dating. Now, I can take you home if you'd like? Or you're welcome to join us for dinner. I can't promise it'll be any good, but still, you're most welcome. I think we're having homemade pizza, which should suit your current condition."

"I'd love to," Kate replied quickly.

"Now Kate," Mum said as we all squeezed into the tiny kitchen upstairs, "what toppings would you like?"

Mum had gone overboard with the options.

"Ah, everything I suppose. I'm not fussy."

"Capsicum?"

"Oh, definitely, I love capsicum."

"See Sam, that's what normal people are like," Mum said, laughing.

"I don't understand?" she asked quizzically.

I know I've already covered my dislike of capsicum previous, but my point here is that the last thing I needed was my mother making an issue out of it in front of my girlfriend.

"Sam can't stand capsicum. Or pretty much any other food. Sometimes we wonder how he doesn't starve."

Kate took that as permission to wave a slice of capsicum in front of my face.

"Argh! Get it away!" I gasped, dry retching.

Kate and Mum both laughed as she swallowed the piece of raw capsicum, exaggerating each chew to make me squirm.

"That's truly disgusting," I said, face screwed up.

"Are you interested in being adopted Kate? We could trade Sam in and adopt you."

Kate laughed.

"That's a very tempting offer Mrs Price."

"Apart from breaking your arm with Sam, what else have you been up to over the holidays, Kate?" Dad asked.

"Not a whole lot. Lazing about, mostly. I've been doing a lot of driving practice actually. I'm going for my P's next week."

"Can you convince Sam to get off his butt and sort out his learners?"

"I can certainly incentivise him."

Which was kind of an awkward thing to say in front of my parents. Dinner wasn't any less awkward, as you might imagine. Kate and I sat a chaste distance apart on the upstairs lounge while watching TV and eating the pizza. Because that's how my laidback parents were about things like that. Mum and Dad pretended not to be nosey while clearly being just that. Kate played her part well at least and she seemed genuinely happy with the conversation she and mum where having about the TV show that was on. I didn't know the show, but they both seemed familiar with the series. Perhaps I was the only one who felt awkward.

We were downstairs and away from them as quickly as politeness allowed. Possibly a little quicker. Kate half shoved me onto my couch, pouncing onto my lap in one swift movement. She clearly had forgotten that her wrist was plastered up because she nearly took my head off as she went to wrap her hand around my neck. Like a baseball bat to the head, the heavier-than-expected cast clipped me across my ear and gave me an instant headache down the right side of my face.

"Oh shit! I'm sorry."

She laughed, despite my obvious pain. I wasn't upset with her, but I still didn't see the humorous side of the ringing in my ears and throbbing pain in my skull.

"Here, let me kiss it better," she said, playfully kissing me under the ear. "Better?"

Not even a little bit, but there's no way I wanted her to stop.

"Your parents are nice."

"I guess so."

"They are."

"It was kind of awkward though."

"Of course, all first dinners with the parents are. They were still nice."

"When will I get to meet yours?"

"Never, hopefully."

"What's the deal with your parents? You always seem pained whenever they come up."

"Nothing, don't worry about it. Dad's just, well, you're lucky to have nice parents."

"What about your Mum?"

Her lips twisted, uncertain. It was subtle, but her head shook twice. Another sensitive topic?

"I won't be able to stay much longer though. Send me home thinking of nicer things Sam."

"What can I do for you?"

Her face was in front of mine, our noses a hair's breadth apart. Her green eyes pierced through mine, pained and purposeful.

"Push your lips against mine and let me think of nothing else."

As if I could do anything else. It was the first time I led. Up until now, she had always been the initiator. This time, I could feel, she let herself go. Let me take control. It felt like she was giving herself over to me as she left herself exposed, trusting me with her care. It felt good to be so close to her. A new feeling that left me instantly addicted to the desire to experience it as often as possible. And I wanted to do nothing else but wrap her up tightly and promise her I'd never let her get hurt again. I wanted to.

"Thanks a lot for the dinner Mr and Mrs Price. I'm afraid I'm going to have to get home, though, before Dad starts wondering where I am."

"Here, let me drive you home," Mum offered.

"You don't have to do that."

"Don't be silly, it's been a long day for you. And I couldn't let you walk with that broken arm of yours."

"That's sweet of you, but I'll be fine. A broken arm isn't going to stop me."

"But it's dark outside," Dad added.

"Don't worry about me. I don't have far to go. I'll be fine, promise." She pointed a finger at me. "The same goes for you. I'll be fine."

Saying goodbye was even more awkward than dinner. They were watching the whole time with their eyes burning into me. I wanted to scream at them to turn around so we could have even a moment of privacy. It's a little ridiculous that I'd be so embarrassed, looking back, but it was still new and uncertain for me.

"So when are we going to the zoo?" Kate asked.

"When are you going for your driving test?"

"Monday."

""How are you going to drive in your test if you have your arm in a cast?" Dad asked.

"I'll work it out Mr Price. It shouldn't affect me much."

"You know, you didn't mention that you didn't actually have your licence before."

"Meh, close enough."

"Tuesday then? I've got work tomorrow, but does Tuesday work for you?"

"Tuesday sounds good."

She kissed me goodbye on the cheek. There was just enough of a wink to leave me with the knowledge that she did it on purpose to leave me even more embarrassed in front of my parents.

"Goodbye Sam."

And then she closed the door.

Monday Morning December 15th 1997

"Did you really ask her to the zoo?" Zach said.

"Yeah?"

He shook his head.

"So. Completely. Hopeless. Honestly Sam, I don't know what we're going to do with you. But don't you worry, I'll work something out and we'll learn you yet."

"I'm not sure you're the kind of expert I should trust. I'm a little hesitant to follow your advice, all things given."

"Ouch, that's harsh, man," Zach said, pretending to be offended.

"But true," I responded.

Zach had come around in the morning to apologise. A serious apology. He'd never done that before. I was so shocked I asked him if he was terminal or something. He laughed and put it down to a new outlook on life. That, in itself, was odd to hear coming from him. Which meant that something was up.

With nothing better to do that day, we did what we always did; we rode to the sand cliffs of South Beach. Along the way was our usual detour to pick up our usual caffeine fix. At that moment, we were sitting at the top of a sand cliff, discussing philosophy, teenage boy style.

Zach laughed and jumped off the cliff, because why not? Though, calling it a cliff is a bit of a stretch. Really, the ocean had eroded away what had once been tall dune, leaving a raised wall of hard sand above the softer sand at the bottom. We'd come here, say stupid shit and jump off for shits and giggles.

"You want my advice?" he called out from below.

Which was a question he asked a lot. Always rhetorical. His advice, though calling it advice was typically quite the stretch, was the kind of thing one would normally look to avoid, but even if I'd said "no," I knew he was going to give it anyway. Nothing stops him once he gets started. I prepped myself for another lecture in his blunt teenaged male logic.

"Nothing good lasts forever. Enjoy it while the going is good."

Nothing mind-blowing there. He was very much an enjoying-things-in-the-moment kind of guy. I hit the sand beside him moments later. The loose sands at the bottom of the cliff made for soft landings, but this time the sands shifted underneath me, sending me stumbling toward the water. I stumbled three steps before landing face first in the sand. Zach was too busy laughing beside me to help me up.

"Apt really." he said. "Like sand, girls are fickle; at any moment they'll shift and throw you face-first into the dirt."

I rolled my eyes at him. Here we go, I thought.

"I don't think Kate will be like that."

"They're all like that."

"Oh, and you know all about women."

"I've dated more than you."

"The same one multiple times doesn't count."

"Your point, exactly? It's still true," he said as we scrambled up to the top of the cliff again. "Look, all I'm saying is, I can appreciate what you see in Kate with those lovely tits of hers," he said with a wicked grin before jumping off the cliff backwards. As he landed, his legs kicked out from under him and he ended laying spreadeagled on his back. He didn't quite sell the over-dramatization.

"But you have to appreciate that gravity wins in the end. Nothing good lasts forever."

"Dude, that's not cool!"

I jumped beside him and landed perfectly.

"Are you saying you don't think your girlfriend has lovely tits?"

"No."

"No she doesn't?"

"You bastard."

He responded with another wicked grin.

"It's just…" I didn't know how to say what I wanted to say. He sat up and stared at me expectantly.

"Spit it out."

"It's not like that between us."

"Yeah, yeah, of course not. Look, I'm only fucking with you man. Admit it though; she does have a fine pair. I mean, not as good as Lizzie's, but still, pretty damn fine."

His description came complete with a set of unnecessary but otherwise representative hand signs. It was over the top and in no way unusual for him.

"I wouldn't know."

He audibly sighed. "What do you mean you wouldn't know? Are you blind? Can you not see what's right in front of you? You can be such a pussy. Sometimes I wonder about you."

We scrambled back up the cliff again. Boobs again. Boobs were a common topic of discussion with him. While I can hardly deny that boobs weren't a popular subject with most teenaged boys, few were as outspoken about it as he was.

"What do you reckon it is about guys and boobs?" I asked once we'd reached the top, sat down on the edge and caught our breath.

Because, seriously, why not double down on the conversation? He looked at me strangely, as if I'd just asked him why the sky is green or why cows can fly.

"They're boobs?"

"Well yes, but what's the fascination? Picture this," I said.

"Well if you insist," he interrupted, holding back a laugh.

"Oh, shut it will you, seriously. Picture this: Imagine two disembodied breasts without anything else. No body, nothing. I don't know about you, but there's no way that's attractive to me. So why the fascination? I mean, sure she was attractive before I met her, but it's only after I met her that I actually found myself attracted to her. Like, before she was beautiful and sexy and all that, but they're just empty adjectives. She's not just a pretty picture to be looked at and lusted over. She seems so smart and witty. I can't explain it though. It's not as if we've had some massive intellectual conversation. Like, we've discussed philosophy and stuff but nothing too extreme. Still, my brain is insisting on telling me how smart and amazing she is yet at the same time telling me she's nothing like what I'd previously considered a smart girl to be. It's screwing with me, that I'm so used to this idea in my head about what is and isn't beautiful, but fuck me if she isn't the most beautiful person ever. And I can't reconcile that. Like, is it bad that I can't get over how physically beautiful she is? And yes, her boobs are amazing, but it's only because they're a part of her."

His response was to laugh at me. "Are you ashamed of finding the girl you're dating attractive?"

I struggled to answer.

"Don't answer that," he cut me off before I could come up with a response. "Do you really want to know what I think? That's how attraction works, stupid. Like, really works. I mean, whether it's their boobs or their brains, stop thinking about how a girl has to have certain attributes to be attractive. It's not like there's some list where you look at person and tick items one by one off the list and once they reach a certain score you suddenly find them attractive. Attraction is subjective. Everyone is different. You want to know why? Because it's not about what she has. It's about how she connects with you with what she has. Like, you say Kate is smart and that's what you find attractive about her. I call bullshit. What you mean is, Kate is smart, and she and you have connected on some intellectual level and it's that connection that you see as attraction. It's like, when you see some girl who you don't think would get a date in a million years but there she is with some boyfriend and you wonder to yourself, how did that happen? You know how? Somehow, they've found a way to connect. You know? It's whatever works for them. It's completely subjective. What you have to see is that when you say 'I want a girl who is smart' you're being as objectifying as the guy who wants a girl with big tits. If some douchey guy and some bimbo with big tits have found some a way to connect, then wish them luck. Because, on the other hand, if they're just ticking boxes on each other's dating criteria list then they're going to be as unhappy as you are, or should I say were, expecting that the only girls you would date had to meet some vague criteria of intelligence. It's awesome that you've connected with Kate. Enjoy it for what it is. Work on growing that connection. You know, that's why Lizzie and I broke up, we had lost that connection. All I'm saying is; enjoy what you have."

I sat in stunned silence for a moment. Despite himself and his crude style, Zach's advice had caught me completely off guard.

"I don't think I've ever heard you string that many sentences altogether in a row. Where the hell did that all come from?"

He shrugged.

"You're right."

"Of course.

"And I think with her I'm starting to see that."

"We all have this plot in our head about how we think life is supposed to go, but let me tell you, as an author…"

"Wait, hold up. 'As an author?' Now you're bullshitting. Since when are you an author?

"One day I will be."

"You haven't written a word in your life, have you?"

"That's beside the point."

"I'm confident it isn't."

"Look, you're ruining my moment here. Anyway, as I was saying, as an author," he continued, "sometimes you have to kill your plot babies. You know, you have this picture in your head about how your story is supposed to turn out, but sometimes you have to let the plot take a different fork in the road. Sometimes you have to let your favourite characters die. You have to be willing to kill off your preconceived notions so that you can get to the better story that's waiting to shine through."

"How can you go from talking about boobs to that sage advice like this?"

"All my advice is sage advice. It's your problem if you haven't paid attention until now. You want some more?"

He then pushed me off the cliff. I landed face first in the sand.

"Never forget, gravity always wins!" He called out from above, laughing the entire time. I spat out a mouthful of sand. I should have seen that coming. He landed perfectly beside me, still laughing at me as I struggled to my feet and tried to brush off all the sand. The resulting chase after him was pitiful. From both of us. Twenty metres running after him through the soft sand and I was exhausted. He fared worse, breathing heavily on his back not three metres in front of me. He could have been miles away for all it mattered because my legs were like jelly. He was still laughing his head off.

"Let's deviate away from my girlfriend's boobs for a moment," I said as we stumbled back toward the sand cliffs again together, "do you really want to be an author?"

He nodded. "Sure."

"I never knew that."

"There are lots of things you don't know about me."

"Do you think you and Lizzie will ever get back together?"

"Haven't you been paying any attention? Bloody hell, for somebody so smart, sometimes you can be so stupid. Come on, let's head, I have to get ready for work."

"For a while there I wasn't sure you were going to return," Kate called out as she hung out of a window on the second storey of my house. Her presence was completely unexpected.

"What are you doing here?" I called back.

"Waiting for you to get back, obviously."

I raced up my house's external stairs. She met me at the front door.

"Guess what?" she said excitedly.

"What?"

"I passed!"

"You passed?" I asked, confused.

"I passed my driving test, silly. I can drive legally now."

"Oh! Well done."

"Come on. We're going out. Grab a towel and some swimmers. My friends and I are going to the beach and you're coming with."

"We are?" I wasn't sure I liked the idea of doing anything with her friends. Nothing against them, I just didn't know any of them. And that meant awkwardness, pretend acceptance and all that other pseudo friendship stuff that typically wasn't much fun for the socially introverted.

"Yes, yes you are. And Zach, you're welcome to come too. We can swing past your place on the way so you can get some gear."

"I'm supposed to work this afternoon," he said, shaking his head.

"Well that sucks. Though I guess Lizzie wouldn't be too happy with you spending the afternoon at the beach with all my hot friends in bikinis anyway."

Zach responded by mocking a coughing fit. "Mind if I borrow your phone Sam?"

"You know where it is."

"Thanks," he said, grinning as he ran into the kitchen.

Kate flashed me a questioning look. "I was being serious about Lizzie."

"Oh, it's a long story."

"Oh dear. Oh well." She grabbed my arm and pulled me inside. "Come on then. Swimmers, go put some on. Hurry, we're already late."

I rushed to my room and turned it upside down looking for something I could wear swimming. That was a problem because I couldn't actually remember the last time I'd gone swimming. Sure, I'd go to the beach with Zach, but actual swimming? That involved getting wet and shit. Real physical activity. Obviously not my thing. And now she wanted me to come and meet her friends, her exceptionally hot friends, in the process?

"Hurry up already. What the hell is taking so long?" she called out.

At which point I knew there was no getting out of it. I resolved to go, and tried to steel myself for how awkward it was going to be. Meeting her friends hadn't even occurred to me before. What the hell was she getting me into? Shit, I thought, was she crazy. How are they going to take to me, the nerdy unattractive kid with absolutely nothing in common?

The board shorts I'd found still fit, amazingly enough. I added an old shirt, well past its use-by date that I thought would be adequate. I grabbed a change of clothes off the floor and with all those, tentatively walked from my room, hoping I had dressed suitably.

Arms overloaded, I copped a thrown towel to the face straight out of my bedroom door. Blinded, I stumbled into her.

"What took you so long?" Kate asked, pulling the towel off my head and grabbing my hand.

"It's been a while."

She peeked over my shoulder.

"Judging by the state of your room, I assume by that you mean it's been a while since you've seen the floor of your room."

"Since when did you become my mother?"

"If you don't hightail it to my car in quick time I'll send you crying to your mother," she responded.

"Hah, I like her," Zach chimed in.

"How the hell exactly did you manage to get your license?" Zach questioned apprehensively. He gripped both the front seats tightly as he leant forward from his place in the middle of the rear seat. Kate thumped the gear stick with her cast until it found the next gear. The car bounced down the road. I wasn't completely convinced the problem was her cast.

"Oh, the instructor is Erin's father. I told her that I wouldn't be able to pick her up to go to the beach if I didn't get my licence. I guess she really wanted to go."

"You blackmailed the driving instructor's daughter?"

"If only. I scraped past in the end. I think he went easy on me because of my cast."

Zach suddenly disappeared as Kate tossed the car around the corner of my street. An indecipherable stream of profanities came from behind Kate's seat as he tried to pull himself up again. I couldn't help but laugh as she swung the car around another corner just as he semi-righted himself, only to watch his head swing in an arc across the backseat and end up somewhere under my seat.

"Not wearing a seatbelt can be deadly," Kate said facetiously.

"Especially with you driving," I added.

Kate flashed me with a dirty look, before poking her tongue out at me. "I can turn around, drop you both off at home and go to the beach with my hot friends all by myself if you'd rather not be in my car?" she said.

"Don't you dare," Zach grumbled.

We all laughed.

Kate hit the brakes hard. Hard enough that my head was almost introduced to the dashboard the hard way. Judging by the stream of profanities that came from the back seat, Zach fared worse. I was starting to get the impression that getting in the car with Kate driving was putting your life in the gods' hands.

The million dollar houses on either side of the street meant we were somewhere in Victoria Bay, an exclusive suburb on the north end of the town for the rich, and a place I'd rarely had reason to visit. Stunned and prone against the dashboard, I caught a flash of two girls running up to the car but they were out of my vision before I saw who it was. Then Zach suddenly stopped swearing, mid fuck. I mean, obviously not mid fuck, but that he choked on the c as if he'd suddenly lost the ability to speak, as if somebody had tugged on an invisible choker leash around his neck. Which wasn't too far from the truth, it turned out. The change in him was sudden and unexpected. After fumbling with his seat belt, he reached over and did something I'd never seen him do before; he opened the car door for somebody. This from a guy who, in his own words, firmly believed that chivalry died in the middle ages. Then he slid back to the other side of the car and sat watching the door, patient and expectant, like a child on his best behaviour. It was so unusual of him it was freaky.

Erin stepped into the car first, almost bouncing her way into the middle seat. She was another classmate from school that had more or less passed me by completely. No reason for it, our paths had simply never crossed until today. She wore a light blue string bikini top that held nothing back and white board shorts patterned in a pink floral print that was popular.

"Hi!" she said with unexpected exuberance.

"Hello!" Zach replied, subtly louder that his usual self. Enough for me to notice. Instantly enamoured, which, unlike everything else, was in no way atypical. I silently wished him luck because I figured he had zero chance with her.

And then she swept into the car and stole my heart's next beat. Despite the fears I had with meeting Kate's friends, I was completely unprepared for her. In contrast to Erin's bubbly entry, Amy somehow managed to be smooth and sophisticated even in her half-buttoned cotton shirt and black board shorts. She wore her pitch-black hair tied into an asymmetric braid swung over her left shoulder and she instantly cut herself into my consciousness.

I took a breath. I waited for the crushing anxiety to abate. I took another breath. She smiled at me and adjusted herself into the seat. There was a conflict raging in my mind. She was no different, still beautiful. My mind was remembering all that I'd imagined about her. It didn't mean anything anymore.

Love is weird. Lust is weirder. Of course, that whole time it would have looked as if I was staring dumbstruck at her. Actually, let's be honest here. I was actually staring dumbstruck at her. One of those stares that transcends well into creepiness. Not intentional, but I'm sure I looked the complete opposite of what was going through my mind. I caught the beginning of her reaction to me. It all started in slow motion, as the voice in my head screamed at me to 'act normal'. But I wasn't able to move. Kate must have noticed because she reached out to touch my leg. It was an awkward touch. Or maybe it was apologetic. I wasn't sure which, because, for all I knew, I could have just been projecting.

"Driver! To the beach!" Erin yelled. Thankfully oblivious.

"And in one piece, please," Zach added. That got both girls in the back laughing. The tension slipped away.

"Seriously though," Amy said, "are you sure you should be driving with that cast on?"

That was the first time I'd really heard Amy speak. Not exactly first time, but close enough such that I'd never noticed her British accent before. She had been new to the school last year, so I guess that suggests where she came from. An interesting coincidence, considering I'd not long confided in Zach my penchant for British accents.

"Don't go there," Zach said deadpan, to more laughter.

Which was good advice. Kate gave the brakes a little tap. Zach swore. Only I was able to see the playful smile her lips made. Her eyes told a different truth.

Monday Afternoon December 15th 1997

Zach and Erin chatted animatedly the entire trip, which I took as a sign Fate was telling me to butt out of things I knew nothing about. Not that I could hear what they were talking about over the music on the radio, but there was no doubt they were having fun. Amy spent most of the trip talking to Kate. I could barely make out their conversation over the radio, but it may as well have been in French for all I could understand. In the end, I tuned out for most of the trip up the coast; my attention spent counting the rows of pines in the kilometre after kilometre of forestry plantations. I couldn't get Amy out of my head. I mean, these plantations had all the right greens and browns. But so impossibly perfect. Artificial nature. I discovered I was holding her hand halfway along the trip.

We pulled off the highway sometime later, and travelled briefly through a town I didn't recognise before turning down a dirt road as we passed the outskirts. The end of the road opened out into a secluded dirt cul-de-sac that served as the parking area for our destination beach. I wish I could claim that I wasn't sure where we were simply because I'd been to so many beaches that I didn't recognise this particular beach, but let's be honest, as if I were going to recognise any beach we might have ended up at. There were at least twenty cars crammed into that little car park, so it seemed a popular place. Everything thumped to a stop as Kate located the park fence with the car's bumper.

"Look," Erin pointed to a red VL Commodore that looked like it had far too much money pumped into it. "That looks like Chris's car. They must be here already."

As I stepped out of the car, two things were immediately obvious. First, it was fucking hot. Second, it was fucking bright. Between barely split eyelids, I could just make out a dodgy looking convenience store slash takeaway shop at the edge of the car park. Beside it ran a broken path that lead from car park to the beach. The path looked like the only way to get to the beach, because banks of sand dunes cut off any other beach access. The group began heading toward the takeaway shop, so I stumbled after them, squinting in the bright sunshine.

"What's up with you?" Kate asked me.

"Sun is disagreeing with me. Can't see a thing."

"Here, stupid," she said, taking off her sunglasses and slipping them onto me.

Zach took one look at me and burst out laughing. "Oh hey there sexy."

"You aren't mocking my sunglasses are you Zach?" Kate said.

"No ma'am, just Sam."

"Oh, that's ok then."

"Hey!"

"Hey, is anyone hungry?" Zach asked.

We had just reached the takeaway shop. There were nods all around.

"If you all chip in some cash, I thought we could get us all a couple of dollars' worth of chips and some bread. If that's cool with everyone?"

"Sure, I'm up for that," Amy answered while the rest of us nodded our agreement.

"Hey, I'm going to grab a drink while we're here, you want anything?" Kate asked me.

"Nah, I'm ok for now."

Kate slipped off my arm to be first into the shop with Zach not far behind. Erin followed close behind Zach, though by 'followed', I mean it was a lot closer to sneaking, as if she expected it would go unnoticed. That left Amy and me alone outside. I opened my mouth to talk to her. Nothing came out. I closed it again. She didn't seem to notice. Or she ignored me.

Same difference. We both stared at nothing, and spoke as much, for the next five minutes. We had that in common, at least.

They finally came out, laughing their heads off at something Zach had said, if I were to hazard a guess. Erin still hung off his every word, which I thought was crazy.

"I know you said you didn't want anything, you said these are hard to find, so I bought you one," Kate said as she passed me a bottle of Jolt.

I'm sure I must have been beaming in that moment, her little gesture dragging me out of my negative thoughts, if just for a moment.

"Can't be too hard to find if you can get them way in here in the middle of nowhere," Amy quipped snidely.

"And for you," she said to Amy as she passed her a can of one of the, still new to the scene, energy drinks. "One impossible to find can of V."

I shook my head at Amy, mocking disapproval, though I hadn't thought the joke completely through. She looked at me weirdly.

"What?" she asked confused.

"Heretic." I tsked.

"What?" She said, still puzzled. "I like the taste."

"Really?" I responded, twisting my face in disgust and thereby digging myself deeper into the hole.

"Yeah. Really." She said, stiff.

"You're both as bad as each other." Kate said with a massive grin.

"Come on guys." Zach cut in loudly. "There are chips and sand and water and beautiful girls in…" He let the sentence trail off.

"You idiot." I shook my head.

He was grinning ear to ear. Everyone laughed at him, even Amy.

Making our way down to the beach was bloody annoying. Whoever built the stairs had decided it'd be great to space each sleeper a few inches too far apart to be walked down easily in single steps but not quite far enough apart to take them in two which made for an awkward shuffle all the way down the 100 metres or so to the bottom. My guess was that the builders were probably off in the distance watching us and laughing their heads off in sadistic pleasure at the people stumbling awkwardly down.

The little beach was packed. Lifeguards, their presence somewhat surprising given that beach seemed to be in the middle of nowhere, had still made the small beach even smaller by setting up the tiniest of areas in the middle with their flags.

I couldn't work out what made that section of the beach different to the rest, but the sand behind the flags was covered in towels and a vast array of people occupying them. We found Chris almost dead centre of the crowd.

With him was a who's who of the popular crowd at school. His girlfriend, Samantha, blonde and magazine perfect, sat close beside him. Next to them were his followers, or his cult worshipers, as we used to joke in school. Chris would never be seen without Justin and Daniel, and Wil and Shane were never far behind, though it seemed that day at least that they had managed to break free from the clutches of the cult, because both had managed to acquire girlfriends. I didn't recognise the girls. Though they weren't twins, the two girls looked so similar with their long cascading blonde hair and blue eyes that it was like Wil and Shane shared notes when deciding to date these girls. Regardless, they still stuck closely to the completely stunningly hot bodies theme that the group had going for it. Zach and I clearly were the odd ones out.

We awkwardly squeezed our towels in next to theirs. I didn't get why we didn't all shift and set up somewhere a little less crowded than this little section of the beach. Zach laid the packet of chips open in the centre of the group and flicked a loaf of bread down next to it. There was a moment of awkwardness as everyone waited for somebody to make the first move. Zach shrugged and opened up the bread. And then it got crazy. A mass of hands as all ten of us acted half-starved as we started devouring these chips. And nobody had said a word yet. Everyone was looking at Zach and me. We were definitely strangers. I guess they didn't know what to make of our presence.

"Good chips, thanks guys. Good call with the chicken salt," Chris said, finally breaking the silence. "What took you guys so long to get here?"

Amy pointed to Kate's cast. "Kate finally found the one thing that can put a dint in her speed addiction."

"Damn, and she still drove?"

"I wouldn't go there if I were you." Zach playfully said. 'That's playing with fire."

"Hey!" Kate responded.

Kate reached over me and swung at him with her cast, playfully, but there was enough intent behind it to have me ducking out of the way. He easily dodged out of the way. She shuffled closer, jumping over me for another attempt but he shifted further and dodged again. He had the biggest grin on his face. She stood up, scowling. Arm raised, she took a step toward him. He bolted. We were all laughing our heads off at them as she chased him all the way to the surf and back again.

"I've got to stop doing this," he huffed, hopping around us as he tried to slip his shoes off while avoiding her. She played into the game, stalking him around the circle, jumping closer each time he tried to stop a moment to untie his laces. He managed his left shoe ok, but his right was his undoing, as he face planted rather melodramatically into the sand, a little conveniently, I think, next to Erin. Ironically, his dive earned him a minor reprieve, with Kate laughing too hard at him to catch up. Erin leant over and helped Zach untangle himself, helping him pull off his other shoe. A friendly pat on his back and a shake of her head signalled the end of the truce. Everyone cheered Zach on as he raced off, back down toward the water. He made his escape, still fully clothed, diving into the water just as she was within clutching distance. She stood on the shore unwilling to follow him in and crossed her arms in mock frustration. Then, though still with a massive smile on her face, she acted out her defeat, shrugging as she walked back to the group.

"Winner!" Zach yelled out from the water.

"Your time will come!" She yelled back.

But it worked to break the ice. The rest of the group were still laughing as they started getting ready to swim. Kate sat down next to me, her breathing heavy as she relaxed against me to catch her breath.

"Well? Are you going to jump in?" she asked me.

"What about you? How are you going to swim with your cast?"

"The doctor told me I should get this special high tech device so that I would be able to get wet and not have any issues." She reached into her bag and pulled out a plastic bag and a roll of electrical tape.

"That really seems like not a great idea, going swimming with that cast on." Amy said.

"Meh, fuck it," Kate said as she slipped her arm into the bag and handed me the tape. "Help me out, will you?"

After I'd taped the bag up tightly, she stood up to strip down to her swimmers. But as she pulled her shirt up over her head, it tangled up, with the cloth caught on her cast and her arms twisted up above head. I admit I may have laughed a little as she stumbled around helplessly. She struggled for a few more seconds, but somehow only managed to make things worse.

"Ah, some help please?"

Shit. Here I was laughing stupidly at my girlfriend as she struggled instead of helping her out. Talk about feeling stupid. Yeah, I was a terrible boyfriend. I jumped up to help her out. We struggled together for a moment but I eventually managed to untangle her. The process left her with her arms around my neck.

"Thanks," she whispered, honest and oblivious to my thoughts.

"Sorry, I…" I started to apologise.

Her lips cut my words short. A short moment grew longer. A boy became quite self-conscious. And I wanted to pull away, away from the false embarrassment, away from the self-exposure. She felt my panic and responded by holding me firm, firm until it dawned on me; what did I have to fear from the eyes looking at us? What did I care about their view on our love? Our love? Another wave crashed as her bottom lip pressed against mine again. The wave washed against the shore until the ripple reached its zenith, a whisper as her lips finally slipped away. Another lesson learnt.

"Well are you going to take that shirt off or what?" she asked.

"Ah, I think I'll leave it on." I didn't feel comfortable without a shirt on. Not in public. I'm hardly the fittest of guys. I'd hoped, naively, to slip pass any embarrassment.

"What's to be embarrassed about? It's just skin. Shit, if all the girls here are willing to take their shirts off, what are you worried about?"

Of course, that comment simply made me painfully aware that I was now seeing my almost half-naked girlfriend, in only a bikini, for the first time. Painfully aware. Without the shirt to mask her body, well, I'm going to withhold describing exactly what I saw, but needless to say, I went straight back to being embarrassed. She was stunning. It also didn't take her long to work out the source of my rather rosy cheeks.

"Just wait until I let you look at them without the bikini," she said so that only I could hear. My jaw may as well have it hit the sand. She giggled.

138

"Come on, arms up," she said tugging on the bottom of my shirt.

I submitted. A kiss stole any resistance I might have put up; it left me, quite literally, weak at the knees. My shirt was off before I realised what had happened.

"Woah, bloody hell, who turned the lights on!" Chris exclaimed. "Put it away, put it away."

Which had the effect of making sure everyone's attention was pointed my direction. The reactions were brutal. The ones where people actually physically recoiled were particularly harsh. It was as cloud free day and the sun was bright, ok?

"I'm just fucking with you," Chris added, laughing. "It's all good. Though a bit of a sun isn't going to do you any harm." He threw a bottle of sunscreen to me. "Don't burn to a crisp."

A few sunscreen bottles made their way around the group. The excessively thick lotion served only to turn me even whiter, if that were even possible. After thoroughly coating every exposed bit of skin I could reach.

"Here, let me do the rest," Kate said, taking the bottle of me.

The sunscreen was cold as her hands gently spread it over my back. She seemed purposefully to take her time, her soft hands seemingly more interested in exploring my body than any real attempt to rub in the sunscreen. It was a real shiver down the spine moment. She was enjoying it. I wasn't sure what had gotten into her, but at that point in time I wasn't looking forward to standing up.

She stopped eventually. I guess she had apparently finished. She had been thorough. I prepared myself for what had the potential to become much more embarrassing moment, with us all about to stand up. You probably get the picture. I was on the cusp of feeling I could get away with things. It could have gone either way. It seems she had other ideas, as if she wouldn't be happy until I was sure to embarrass myself. She handed me the bottle, crawled over me and sat down between my legs with her back to me.

"Now do me."

It was the kind of off the cuff phrase straight out of a bad teenage fantasy. Well, let's be honest, straight out of one of my own fantasies. Except for the beach scene. I probably wouldn't have placed it in a beach scene. Minor detail.

'Don't panic!' the voice in my head screamed.

Except the voice wasn't having the desired effect because I completely froze up.

'You've got this'.

'No I don't'.

'Just wing it.'

'It's not working'.

'You're taking too long, she's starting to notice.'

'She's your girlfriend, stupid'.

That was a new voice. And it hit me hard.

"You're good at that," she whispered.

It came as a surprise to find my hands on her back. Apparently that voice was the subconscious kick I needed. Whether I was doing it right or not, she felt good. I gave some mumbled noise in response.

She tilted her head back, showing off a massive grin.

"I am rather enjoying this."

"You are?"

"Teasing you, that is," she whispered.

"I can barely think straight,"

"A little too much perhaps? Sorry."

"Don't be, I'm just…"

"No, don't stop. Relax. It feels good."

"Seriously guys, are you coming in or what?" Zach shouted out from the water.

"Sorry babe," Kate said to me with an exaggerated pout. "But I have to go sort that boy out."

"Just don't hurt him."

"I make no promises," she yelled back at me as she ran down the beach.

Moments later, Chris and the other guys surrounded me as I walked toward the water.

"So how'd you do it?" he asked in hushed tones.

"How'd I do what?" I responded, confused and far less quietly.

"Shhh, not so loud. Seriously though, how'd you do it? How'd you tame the untameable?"

Forgive my innocence a moment here, because I didn't have a clue what he was talking about. He nudged me, I realise now, presumably thinking I was trying to avoid answering. And then it clicked. Why the hell would her friends suggest that of her? And what was I supposed to do here? They weren't interested in anything remotely close to the truth.

So things got awkward. That was the kind of shit I'm not good at dealing with. I lied. And I regretted my response immediately. A part of me didn't want to. A big part of me didn't want to. It was a panicked response. A crude joke let them hear what they expected to hear. And no, I'm not going to cover off what it was, but I wasn't proud of myself. Worse, it seemed to break down a few more of the barriers between us. Things were more relaxed among us from that moment on. Which made me feel like absolute shit.

I walked into the water with that still on my mind when a football manifested itself in my arms. I had barely had time to recognise what it was when suddenly I found myself sucking down salt water. And thus went my first taste of mugby, a game where whoever has the ball is 'it' and pretty much anything else goes. Like tag, with added violence.

The ball passed back and forth between the others until, noticing a moment of laxity from Wil, I slyly stripped the ball while his attention was toward the others. I ran for it, enjoying the brief success. It didn't last long. My brain decided that then was a good time to contemplate the conflicting ideals of being accepted by the very people who would never have given me the time of day during the school year with the fact that frankly, I wasn't sure I actually wanted it. Then it told me to stop being a hypocrite and enjoy the moment.

That lasted all of five more seconds when Samantha near snapped me in half with an impressive tackle, casually took the ball from my hands, and practically dared me to try to take it back. Which wasn't remotely fair; I was too scared to touch her, given that Chris was the biggest guy on the football team and, from what I could tell out of the corner of my eye, looking for any excuse to become involved.

Kate wandered back up the beach to sit with Amy and it seemed to me like a good excuse to catch my own breath. Amy hadn't moved from her spot the entire time here, instead reading from a book in a scene that I would have mirrored any other time.

"Why don't you join us?" I asked Amy between breaths. I must have been pretty hyped, because at that moment I didn't think twice about talking to her.

She gave a quick shake of her head and held up the book she was reading, as if I couldn't already see it, thick and ancient, gilded and with the gold lettering in the style those old books tended to be. The title said *Anna Karenina*, which, in my eyes, well suited the pretentiousness of such a styled book.

"Amy doesn't do that. Not into the physical stuff." Kate explained.

'Neither was I' I felt like saying, but instead let the conversation drop.

"But you're enjoying yourself?" Kate asked.

"Yeah,"

"See, I told you so." She ruffled my hair, as a grandmother might do to a young child. Then her attention went to the water and she grabbed my wrist excitedly.

"Oh, we have to get involved with that!" she said.

Everyone else was back in the water. Zach disappeared under the water for a moment as Erin slid upon his shoulders. Wil and his girlfriend were doing the same opposite them. And then the match was on, with water flying everywhere, as the two girls wrestled to claim victory. Moments later, Wil's girlfriend took a dive off his shoulders, losing to Erin with a giant splash. The rest of the group cheered their win, though Zach appeared less happy, as the water Erin kicked up half drowned him.

"Have fun," Amy said with a roll of her eyes.

"Come on," Kate said excitedly, ignoring her.

Once in the water, Kate skipped the formalities of getting me to duck under the water as she half jumped half crawled onto my back. Foregoing waiting our turn or anything remotely in order, our first 'match', that is whoever happened to be closest to us at the time, consisted less of anything remotely per any rules and more of what was in reality an uncontrolled fall as Kate launched us, with me completely unprepared, toward Samantha and Chris. It ended predictably; my prize – water up my nose and stinging salt in my eyes.

Despite this, despite my earlier trepidation, jumping into the ocean and letting go had turned an afternoon into a lot of fun. It was something I'd never expected these holidays. We stayed on the beach in one form or another until the sun threatened to end the afternoon regardless of our own desires.

Chris came up to speak to me. "Hey, it's been cool having you here," He said.

"It's been a lot of fun,"

"Yeah, I gotta admit, I wasn't sure when I saw you guys arrive, but you're cool, it's been fun. Anyways, I'm holding a massive house party at my place tonight, trying to get as many people there as possible, you interested?"

"Of course we are." Kate jumped in, before I could answer otherwise. She flashed me a devious grin, for my eyes only.

The truth though was that I was interested. As you might imagine, house parties weren't my thing either, but I was on such a high from the afternoon that I felt ready to try anything.

"Yes well, we know you're always in, Kate. My old man is supplying, so feel free to rock up whenever you like."

And with that, the afternoon was over. As we all tracked back to the cars, the reality of spending far too long in the sun kicked it. We were all as red as Kate's red car. There might have been another lesson in that. Remember to keep applying sunscreen.

"Hey, some warning next time you're going to be home late, yeah?"

"Sorry Mrs Price. It's my fault. We kept him out too late."

"I'll forgive you this time, but only because I like you Kate."

"I hope you don't change your mind when I tell you we plan on heading straight out to a party tonight."

"I should probably thank you for actually getting him out of the house for once. Sam, don't hesitate to call us if you need anything, don't go getting into cars of people who have been drinking. That includes you, Miss Kate. I've stuck your dinner in the fridge, you can have it tomorrow."

"It's ok. We'll be walking, but thanks Mrs Price."

With subtle push, she signalled our chance to get away.

"Go have a quick shower and get changed. I'll wait here for you to get ready. Then we'll head back to my place so I can get out of these beach clothes."

Monday Night December 15th 1997

Kate's house was, to put it nicely, modest. The small, dilapidated place, complete with a well-faded white picket fence and front lawn a few months shy of a lawn mower, was not at all what I had expected her place to be. It almost made my half-renovated mess of house look up-market. Almost. I don't know why I assumed that she lived in a nicer place. I guess, with the nice clothes she wore and the company she kept, I'd assumed her family was better off. You'd have thought I'd have learnt to stop making those sort of assumptions by then.

She hesitated as we walked up to her front gate. Not a momentary hesitation but a major crisis kind of hesitation.

"What's up?" I asked.

"Would you mind waiting outside while I got ready?"

"Sure, no problem." It didn't occur to me that this was a weird request of her to make.

"Sorry, I just…"

"No worries." I replied, still unaware what the issue was.

"Ah, fuck it, you might as well."

"I don't mind."

"Sorry, it's not you, it's just…" she hesitated. "Look, don't worry about it. Come on in."

The inside of the house looked like it never made it out of the 80's, a mismatch of furniture and texture that somehow lent the house a warm if overwhelmingly dull homeliness. Kate seemed to make a conscious effort to close the heavy front door quietly, though the rotating lock still made a distinct click as the striker hit home. She paused a moment, waiting to see if she was heard.

"Is that you Kate? Where the hell have you been?" a heavy male voice called from deep within the home.

Kate flinched, mouthing the word 'fuck' to herself. I get that meeting the parents can be scary, but I wasn't sure what she had to be so concerned about. I was the one doing the meeting for the first time. It should be said that I hadn't actually thought about it until then. So, the nervousness hit as her father stepped into room.

"Kate, didn't you hear…" He started. "Oh."

"So Dad, this is Sam,"

"Well, that explains a lot," he said, taking me in with what appeared a genuine smile.

He reached his massive hand out. He was huge, scary huge. He had the body of an old biker, heavy set and formidable, yet far from the point of corpulence, with a thick unkempt beard of wiry white and tree trunks for arms covered in archaic tattoos.

"Pleasure to meet you Sam."

"Nice to meet you too, Sir."

"Sir? You had better stop that nonsense pretty quickly. Dave is fine. Are you staying for dinner?"

"We're not staying Dad," Kate jumped in with, "I came home because I needed to change clothes."

There was a strange tension between the two of them; pleasantries staged for my benefit. Kate's body language was overflowing with awkwardness. At least, that's what I thought I was seeing. My guess, perhaps biased by his demeanour and physicality, was that her father was perhaps a little on the strict side and perhaps the two of them didn't get along. Standard parent/teenager stuff. That was something I understood. Though in that regard, I thought I'd scored pretty well with my own parents. Most of the time.

"Don't worry. I'll keep Sam entertained while you sort yourself out. You watch the cricket Sam? How about a beer? You look like you could use one. Grab a seat in the lounge room and I'll bring you a beer."

Beer and cricket? Was that all she was worried about? I could appreciate that she had my best interests in mind by trying to avoid putting me in a situation she knew I wouldn't enjoy, but surely she wasn't worried about leaving me here for what was only a short period. I was sure I could survive at least a short time. How long was she expecting it to take her to get ready?

I set myself down on a flowery and rather well used couch and tried to work out what was going on in the cricket. The yellow team, apparently Australia, were fielding, while the blue team were batting. Kate's father returned before I could work out who the blue team was, cracking open a can of Australia's cheapest as he handed it to me.

"So how long have you two been dating?" he asked as he sat down.

Shit, I thought to myself. I could survive beer and cricket, but *this*? Silently, I started desperately wishing for Kate to hurry.

"A week or so," I quickly replied. "Not long I guess."

"Yeah well, I think you should know, you hurt my daughter I'll fucking kill you."

My reaction was as you'd expect it to be. I shit myself. Figuratively, not literally. Though there was definitely a tense moment where I wasn't completely sure of that. And where the fuck did that come from? Awkward I thought I could cope with, but that was too much, I wasn't prepared for that.

And then it dawned on me that the glare I thought I saw was actually a poorly hidden smirk. He burst out laughing at me.

"Your face… I ought to do that more often. Best laugh I've had in a while. I'm only fucking with you mate," he said, pausing a moment to laugh at me further. "Relax, it was a joke. Mind you, the bit about not hurting her is true. Still…"

Thankfully, the cricket on TV interrupted this unnerving conversation. Apparently the yellow team, which I was reasonably confident by that stage were Australia, had done something worth celebrating. I joined in half-heartedly with Dave's celebration, half so that it didn't stand out that I had no idea what was going on and half with a hope that it would kill of our conversation.

The cricket gods must have been listening to my silent prayers, because we sat out the rest of the time in silence, him thoroughly engrossed in the sport and me struggling my way through that horrid beer, barely successful in supressing contortions my face kept trying to pull.

There is this myth that every girl must spend forever getting ready, a myth that would have served to make my current situation even more of a struggle were it not for the fact that I had zero previous experience in this area. Truth be told, it blew me away how amazing she looked, in as little time as she spent getting ready. Moreover, she did it in less time than I would have taken. Later, she would go on to describe what she wore as 'simple' and 'boring' but right then she was anything but.

"Ready?"

In all honesty? Probably not.

"When are you going to be home?" Kate's father asked.

Kate shrugged.

"Going to give me a hint?" He waited for an answer.

"Not late Dad."

"See it isn't past midnight."

"Ok Dad," she said, taking my hand and leading me toward the front door.

I probably wouldn't have rolled my eyes so blatantly in front of my father, even if my back were turned. We rushed out the door as quickly as possible.

I'll admit to never being part of the local party scene. Not then and still. I don't think that comes as any surprise. Didn't have the friendship circle to be invited to the big ones. Given my own predilections, that had suited me well enough. Most of my knowledge on the subject was bad American teenage comedy movies, and I suspected they might not have revealed the entire truth. As we arrived at Chris's place though, it appeared he was trying his best to live up to that trope. His house, the polar opposite of Kate's, was huge. It was a massive multi-storey upmarket place on the Port Bay canals, done in the pseudo-Mediterranean style that was popular in this area. I found it gaudy and overdone. The place was crawling with people all through the house as thumping music was barely drowned out by the drone of too many loud conversations. Kate grabbed my arm and together we plunged into the mass. From time to time, as we shuffled through the house, I'd recognise somebody from school, but there we so many people here who I didn't recognise. They might have been from other schools, but I thought I at least knew by sight most of the people in our grade around town. It made me wonder where they all came from.

"Sam, Sam, my man, you have to help me." Zach said he spotted us. He rushed over and pulled me aside. I think his intention was to get me out of hearing distance of Kate, but she listened intently in on our conversation anyway. She showed me a bemused smile as she stood quietly behind Zach.

I couldn't tell if his overly boisterous tone was his usual self or the cheap vodka premix he held in his hand talking. "Firstly, I need you to drink this," he continued, pulling a second can out of his pants and handing it to me. "Secondly, I need you to get me drunk enough to ask Erin out."

"Why do you need to be drunk for that?"

"I don't know man, I'm just…"

"You? Nervous? This is not like you, Zach?"

"I don't get it," Kate said, casually slipping herself into the conversation. "You two were all over each other today. What's different now?"

"I don't know, that was different. Now I've had time to think and it's just…"

"Knowing Erin, I'm sure you have nothing to worry about. Is she here yet?"

"Kate!" Erin shrilled from across the room.

Now that was serendipitous timing. Though judging by Zach's wide-eyed and uncharacteristically nervous stance, he disagreed. Again, completely out of character for him. What a strange reversal. Since when was I the one that would be ok in this situation and he the nervous one? Or… who was I kidding, I would probably have been as nervous were I trying to gather up the courage to ask a girl like Erin out.

Erin and Kate went through this ritual greeting (for lack of a better description) that only girls seem to do, where they hug each other in this jilted and overly dramatic fashion that makes the whole thing look so false. Which confused me, because they looked genuinely happy to see each other. The strange process seemed more about showing off the affection than actually giving it.

I considered for a moment why this process only existed as a girl thing before making the connection that this was exactly the same ritual we guys go through when shaking hands, that awkward process of greeting some person who's name you'll quickly forget where more time is spent on doing it the correct way than actually greeting the person. And that was something I considered as confusing. It's funny how we develop these culturally-specific and gender-specific roles and rituals. They all seemed confusing and pointless. Like most of our social rules, I guess.

Ritual completed, Erin's attention shifted to Zach. She could barely contain her bright smile to him. An expression I was familiar with, when Kate showed me the same. Then she shuffled beside him, slid her arm around his waist and leaned, an action that was completely unambiguous.

"Problem solved," Kate said to nobody in particular.

Zach smiled sheepishly.

We found ourselves amongst a group of strangers who welcomed us into their discussion as if long lost friends. The general theme of the conversation involved a lot of bitching about people who weren't present, with an added serving of salacious rumour. I paid at least some attention to the rumours passed around, for a while at least. They tended to say much more about the teller of the rumour than the subject of it. That led to some interesting insights into the people around us.

I discovered this about parties; they were really just massive group therapy for teenagers. With added alcohol. Which, I'll add, apparently makes me hilarious. My entertainment value was helped along by the cheap vodka premixes that kept appearing out of nowhere, a little too conveniently. I might have paid more attention if not for the fact that alcohol also made me a lot more comfortable with the public display of affection. And Kate was pouring them upon me.

"This isn't working," she whispered about an hour after we'd arrived at the party.

"What isn't working?"

"All these people isn't working. We need to go somewhere where I can forget everyone but you."

Things became heated as soon as we found ourselves somewhere a little away from everything. We ended up on a couch tucked in a corner, no more private than anywhere else in the house, but the atmosphere of this room was more subdued than to the house average. We took the entire couch, me on my back while she lay half over me; her cast awkwardly pressed into my back, though easily disregarded with the help of alcohol. Alcohol, it seems, makes things a little more fluid; the way her tongue flowed between my lips and the way her hands flowed over me. Discrete? We were far from it.

Things on that couch went... further. We carried on for, well, a long time. Don't expect me to remember exactly how long because I lost track of time the moment her lips touched mine. She, with the thin excuse that her back was too sunburnt for my hands to caress, directed my hands to her chest, taking my hands with hers and planting them firmly to her breasts. She didn't give me any chance to protest innocence, her lips thrust firmly against mine before I could utter a word. And why would I complain? Frankly, I was still recovering from the shock of it. I may not have been thinking straight. Can you blame me? I thought she'd been joking earlier. Perhaps I wasn't expecting her to make that sort of move, and make it so blatantly. Surely by then I should have known not to pay attention to what I expected to happen.

Sometime later, relatively speaking of course because I had no idea exactly how long after, out of the corner of my eye, I caught Zach hand in hand with Erin. I had a good view of the internal staircase that spiralled up and paused our current affections momentarily and watched them with some curiosity as they snuck up the stairs and out of view.

"Don't get any ideas from those two. You're staying above the belt tonight, mister."

No, I was happy where I was at that point. Let Zach and Erin do whatever they want, it was their choice. They quickly slipped out of my mind as my focus drifted back to the task at hand.

"You know, it works better with less cloth in between," she mumbled.

Bra - 1, Sam - 0. I fell victim to the bra strap curse that plagues men around the world and prevents them in their moment of need from undoing a simple clasp.

"Here, let me," she said as she managed effortlessly what I couldn't.

She was right. Things were a lot better this way. I drunk in each reaction from her as my fingertips passed over her skin. I focused on the areas that drew even more reaction from her.

I think it best I gloss over the rest of the detail, you get the picture... Needless to say, this carried on for some long time more. This whole while I felt like she was sweeping me away and though the pace of things was quicker than I was ready for, I was glad I had no choice but to let it happen.

"Hey Sam, have you seen Zach? I thought I saw him and I want to talk to him," Lizzie said, her casual question coming as a shock to both Kate and me, given our current activities. I'll add here that she asked this as both my hands were very obviously deep under Kate's shirt and thumbs may or may not have been caressing her, which may not have been as obvious and the exact details of which aren't important but I'm adding them to reflect how unprepared I was to answer any questions at that point in time. I had a fair idea of where Zach was. And that truth was the last thing I wanted to tell her right now. And not because I wanted to protect Zach. His choices were his own to deal with. I was concerned I'd say something and hurt her. That and I didn't know how to deal with the consequences if she found out. I didn't know if I could deal with the consequences. And I was otherwise preoccupied. So I did what everybody else does when presented with a situation worth avoiding. I lied. Or, at best, I told a half-truth. Something to avoid drawing further attention to myself.

"He was around but I haven't seen him in a while," I responded, then tilted my head toward Kate, a hint that I wasn't in a position to help right now.

Lizzie didn't appear to buy into my lie. She peered at us a little closer. A grin spread across her face. If it weren't so dark, I'd imagine I probably would have seen her blushing.

"Oh, I'm sorry for interrupting," she said, giggling to herself. Then her voice became serious, hurt. "But if you see him, can you send him my way? We need to talk."

Getting between them was the last thing I wanted. Worse, I knew that there was nothing I could do that I wouldn't later regret. And there was nothing I could do about that. There was no way things between them would ever end well.

Speaking of not ending well, things soon after went south for Kate. All her heavy drinking caught up with her. Heavy breathing turned into deep breaths and half-composed pauses. She sat up rapidly, shook her head once, swallowed hard, and then bolted.

It wasn't difficult finding her; follow the sound of vomiting. I found her curled over the toilet, violently retching out a night's worth of vodka into her porcelain companion as black mascara streamed down her face.

"I'm sorry," she mumbled.

I sat down behind her and rubbed her back.

"For what?" I replied, trying to offer her what little comfort I could.

"I always do this."

"Do what?"

"Drink too much."

"Don't worry about it."

"You don't understand."

"Really, don't worry about it."

"I'd hoped you wouldn't get to see this side of me. It's all my fault."

"You don't need to hide anything from me."

I had my fingers in her hair, trying to hold it out of the toilet. She lifted her head to give me a smile. It was a miserable and distraught smile, but there nevertheless. It shifted as quickly as she gave it, then she turned and threw up again.

A glass of water was placed on the tiles beside me. Amy stood nonchalantly above us. She shrugged at me, unperturbed. Wil appeared in the corridor behind Amy.

"Making your usual sacrifice to the porcelain god Kate?" he jeered. He looked down at me over Amy's shoulder. "You want my advice? Run. Run as far as you can from that one."

"Oh, fuck off Wil!" Amy yelled and started shoving him away.

"Hey, I'm just giving the man some friendly advice."

"What part of fuck off don't you understand!"

"All right, I'm leaving, I'm leaving."

"Ignore him. Once a wanker, always a wanker," Amy said to me. The first words she'd ever spoken to me. Not how I'd pictured our first conversation together. She kept feeding Kate water while I stayed at her side, waiting for her to work it all out of her system.

It took her about twenty minutes, but Kate eventually recovered enough to stop constantly dry retching.

"Come on, let's get you in a bed," Amy said and together we helped Kate to her feet and started the long journey through the house. Everybody avoided our gaze as we led Kate to the front door. I wanted to scream at them. As if they'd never saw a drunk person before. All the hushed tones and hidden whispers threw me. But fuck them.

We stumbled our way out of the rich suburb. We didn't take the roads I would have expected to take to get back to Kate's place, but Amy seemed confident, so I followed her lead. After about fifteen minutes, Kate started to stabilise enough to walk on her own, with a little assistance. She needed help heading in the right direction and it was slow going the entire time, but we managed. The entire way Amy and I didn't speak; it was just a duty silently shared.

It turned out that Amy wasn't taking us to Kate's house. We ended up walking to the house where we had picked her and Erin up. I'd assumed it was Erin's, but turned out it was Amy's place. Kate had thrown up only twice on the way.

"Thanks, I'm used to having to do that myself," Amy said to me. "It's nice to have help. I'll get her into bed."

"We're not going to her place?"

"And let her Dad see her like this? No. That's not a good idea. And I'm sure she'd rather you didn't have to deal with that. Can you imagine if her Dad caught you with her like this? I think it's best if you leave it at this. I can deal from here."

"Are you sure? Will you be ok with her?"

"Yeah, we've been here before. Goodnight Sam. Thank you for your help tonight. You're different, and she needs that."

Tuesday Morning December 16th 1997

I woke up at 11:13AM. Morning, what was left of it. The sun made sure I knew it was up. My bladder and stomach competed for which could cause me more pain. You'd think I could have sorted out priorities, but my brain hadn't started functioning yet. The stairs made an interesting challenge.

"He's up. Good morning!" Mother shouted at me. Or at least it seemed like it. Her voice smashed through my head. I mumbled some sort of reply.

"Do you have work today?" she asked as I struggled with the simple act of buttering toast.

I responded with another incoherent offering.

"I take it that was a yes. Drink some water, it'll help," she offered.

The water helped, as did the burnt bread. My brain took its time getting back to a level of coherency but a full stomach seemed to help get me functioning. Things were getting better. Except for the sun, which was an unrelenting bastard. And here I'd heard vodka was supposed to be hangover-free. Lies, all lies. I at least had a few hours to recover before work.

My thoughts travelled to Kate. Particularly, I wondered if she'd made it home ok. I hoped she was ok. I considered what Amy said the previous night. The clock on the wall corrected me, telling me it was only a few hours ago. I wasn't sure if I should go over to her place to check up on her, or, for that matter, if she'd even want to see me. And I still didn't have a phone number to call and check. My stomach twisted, telling me that while I might suck as her boyfriend if I didn't check up on her, right then I was in no position to do anything. I crawled back into bed.

Tuesday Night December 16th 1997

"So?"

I was arms-deep in the washing up sink at work when Lizzie entered the prep area, stood with her arms crossed and stared accusingly at me. Shit. My head still thumped painfully. She deserved a better explanation than I was willing to give her, frankly.

"Honestly, I didn't see him after you came to us. Kate got sick not long after you, ah, interrupted us, and we left."

"Damn him."

"Sorry."

"Tell me the truth. Did I see him with another girl at that party or not?"

"I, ah." I fumbled over the words while looking for the nearest window to jump out of.

"I'll take that as a yes."

"Look, I don't know what to say here."

"Don't worry; it's not your fault."

She said it so unconvincingly that I immediately felt like she was blaming me, regardless. And that hurt, despite it making no sense that she was blaming me.

"How are you and Kate going?" she asked, changing the subject. She suppressed a giggle. "I guess that's a silly question, considering what you two were up to last night."

"I guess that means things are good. But I have a question for you." I saw an opportunity to resolve the question I'd been asking myself all morning.

"Shoot."

"I mean, Kate got pretty sick last night; Amy and I walked her to Amy's house and I feel pretty bad today that I haven't checked to see how she's going. What should I have done?"

"Called her, of course."

"And if I don't have her phone number?"

"I suppose that would make calling her hard to do. Yeah, you should probably have gone over to see her. You didn't do that, did you?"

"No."

"You fool. Make sure you apologise next time you see her. And get her phone number, stupid."

"Lizzie! Counter!" our boss yelled out.

She rolled her eyes in frustration and left me pondering the consequences of not visiting Kate sooner.

Wednesday Morning December 17th 1997

I rode over to her place early Wednesday morning intending to make up for my relationship faux pas. That had been the plan, anyway. I arrived at roughly mid-morning. I might have arrived earlier, but I managed to get lost twice along the way. I tapped on her front door and waited expectantly.

"Sorry mate, she's in no position to come out today," her father said, answering the door.

"Oh, why is that? Is she sick or something?"

"Nope, she's in the shit with me and she ain't going anywhere for a while, sorry. I tell you what though; you seem like a nice kid, so I'll let her know you came around. Maybe if she sorts her shit out, she'll be in contact soon."

Which sucked. What kind of bullshit passive aggressive response was that? I drifted off down the road uncertain what I should do next. My thoughts had ground to halt; my brain couldn't comprehend doing anything other than follow the expected path. What the hell was with not letting her out anyway? She was seventeen, not some kid.

"Hey, wait up!" Kate called out as she ran down her street to catch up to me.

Now that really screwed with my head, not going to plan was no longer going to plan.

"Oh hey, aren't you supposed to be grounded or something?"

"Hopefully he doesn't notice."

"Hopefully? Is it going to be a problem?"

"Nah, he'll be too pissed to notice, soon enough."

"It's a bit early for that isn't it?"

"Yeah well… So what are we up to today?"

"Well, I came around to see how you were. And to apologise for being a shit boyfriend and not checking in on you yesterday"

"Apologise? What the fuck for? I'm the one who should apologise to you. Amy filled me in on the details. Thanks for being cool about it; I may have gone a bit overboard. Old habits, bad habits." She ended her explanation with a shrug.

"How's the head?"

"Fine, now. Yesterday wasn't so pleasant though."

"So you're not upset I didn't check up on you?"

"Why would I be? Have you been getting some bad advice mister?"

My hesitation was answer enough for her.

"I'm a big girl Sam. My faults are mine own to suffer through. You don't need to be with me every day. Otherwise, you'll come across as needy, and that's bad. Not that I think you are; just don't define your life by your relationship with me. Now, what did you want to do today? I believe I promised a trip to the zoo with you. Actually, didn't I say we should head there yesterday? Shit, sorry."

"Nah, it's ok, I was hardly in the best shape to do anything either. I ended up spending the whole day in bed. I take it your car isn't an option."

"Yeah, let's try and avoid that option."

"We'll work something out."

Something, in this case, involved sucking up to mother so that she would give us a lift. Apparently, having a girlfriend made this process considerably easier. Mum seemed quite enamoured with Kate, they shared creative souls and I think, in a way, this helped connect them. Sure, Mum played at the lift being such an inconvenience, making a fuss and all, but she was clearly overplaying the part to tease us. There was a moment when I considered how much easier previous requests of her might have played out easier if only I'd met Kate earlier in life. It sure could have saved a few arguments, I mused.

"Are you going to be ok with that arm of yours?" Mum asked Kate as she dropped us off at the zoo's entrance.

"Of course, Mrs Price. Apart from the fact I keep hitting everybody with it, it isn't much of an issue anymore."

"And when did you want to be picked up?" Mum asked.

"When does this place close? Five I guess," I answered.

"Here then, take my mobile phone, in case you need it," she said, handing me her work phone, a massive Nokia, one of the ones that came with the slide out cover but disappointingly not the one that came with snake. "Don't lose that, it's expensive," she said, before she drove off.

"So what do you want to do first?" I asked.

Kate mulled a moment.

"It sucks that I don't have my camera."

"Why don't we visit the gift shop first then, surely they'll have a disposable camera."

Her face twisted on the word 'disposable'.

"It'll better than nothing," I offered.

"I suppose."

Once inside the gift shop, I picked out the disposable camera with the biggest roll of film, thinking that would be the most useful for her. I flinched at the price. Twenty bucks was ridiculously expensive for what was merely a cardboard box with a lens. Damn overpriced gift shops.

A fluffy stuffed animal landed on my shoulder.

"Rawr!" Kate growled.

"What's that supposed to be?"

"It's a rawrasaurus, of course." She scoffed at me. "And you call yourself a dinosaur fan. It's a…" she flipped it upside down to check the tag, "Allosaurus."

She mispronounced it Al-loss-saur-us which made her seem even cuter. I could kind of see the resemblance in the stuffed toy, if I squinted enough. It came from a small shelf titled 'Dinosaurs from Australia' and had a couple of different fluffy dinosaurs to pick from, promoting locally found species like Muttaburrasaurus and Leaellynasaura with fluffy shapes that vaguely referenced them.

"Allosaurus? I think their info is a bit out of date."

"Oh come on mister serious pants, it's cute, look, rawr!"

"Sure, it's cute."

However, it was the price tag that grabbed my attention. What was with these gift shops anyway, how could anybody afford this stuff?

I paid for the camera and abandoned the store as quickly as possible. With my minimum wage job, I couldn't afford the air in that place.

Outside, Kate grabbed me around the shoulders and, with a click, took a photo of us as she kissed me on the cheek.

"I thought you'd be more about taking photos of the animals," I said.

"Are we not all just animals?"

"You know what I mean."

"The camera is all about memories for me."

"So what's the difference then between a disposable and your fancy camera?"

She contemplated the question for a moment. "Good point. I suppose I just wanted my memories with you to be perfect. You have a good point. For once in my life, perhaps the present is more perfect than the memories that can be created. I guess we'll see."

We raced through the zoo, barely stopping to check out any of the animals. While there's no doubt that there are bigger collections elsewhere, our small town zoo still had an impressive collection of exhibits for its size. And it wasn't the other animals' fault that we rushed past them; they simply weren't what we were there for. The zoo had a massive collection of bird aviaries. It was the biggest in the state. We burned through the African animals and barely paused at the local Australian wildlife exhibits. Once past the otters – which did hold our attention for at least a few additional minutes due not in the least to their overabundance of cuteness – and beyond the crocodile pools, which didn't interest us half as much, we bee-lined it toward the birds, which were the final attraction within the zoo.

There, I lost her. I mean, she was standing right beside me the whole time, but she was so enthralled by the bird exhibits she became lost to the world around us. At one point, I tried to remind her that the camera had only a limited number of shots before it would run out and I couldn't afford another. I doubt that even registered as she kept clicking away. I also tried my best to keep up with all the various species she rapidly pointed out in her elation. She led me like an excited child through all the open aviaries, stopping in each to try to get a glimpse of each bird mentioned on the information posts through the aviary.

After the open aviaries, with their parrots and lorikeets and doves and cockatoos, we wandered past a long line of closed aviaries where the zoo kept the species that were less likely to take well to meeting humans. We'd walked down a string of five aviaries in a row when a familiar birdsong paused me. I touched Kate's arm to stop her so we could get a closer look.

"You know, it would have been easier to take a photo of currawongs in here," I said, pointing toward the familiar black bird up in the trees above us. "There are a lot less things for you to fall off."

She whacked me with her cast and then poked her tongue out at me.

"In all seriousness though," she said, "there's something different about photographing something in nature. Don't get me wrong, it's cool we've come out here and I'm glad I get to see these birds up close like this. There's something different though about seeing a bird free in nature that makes the photos so much better. I can't explain."

"I can understand that. This was the best I could do."

"You did well. There's no way I'd get the chance to see so many kinds in one place."

After a line of smaller aviaries, we came to one massive domed aviary that allowed you to walk a complete circle around it, at least twenty metres in circumference.

Inside were finches, wrens, warblers, as well as all manner of species I'd never heard of before. The finches in particularly were a cacophony of noise and colour, and, given the speed at which they moved, I wondered how anybody managed to take the crystal clear photos of them on the information plates.

Tucked diminutively behind the large finch aviary, there was a small cage. A brass information plate stood on a pole in front of the cage, standing off-vertical and looking ready to fall over. It seemed out of place amongst the far bigger aviaries we'd passed through. I read the name 'Superb Lyrebird' etched in bold serif. So imagine my excitement for a moment.

Then, multiply it by a hundred and you'll understand Kate's reaction beside me. This was the whole point of bringing her here, the one bird she was so eager to see. I made a mental note to tell Zach where he can stick his opinions of going to the zoo as a date the next time I saw him. The gamble, I thought, had paid off. We pressed our faces simultaneously against the cage, looking for the elusive lyrebird. What we found was blonde, roughly five foot four and wearing green khakis. Probably around our age. Not exactly what I had in mind.

"Sorry folks, there's nothing here at the moment," the keeper said casually, propped against her rake.

"Why's that?" I asked.

"We, ah, had an incident a few days ago. A snake broke into the cage somehow and well… I don't think you want the details."

"Seriously?"

"Afraid so."

"It's just that we'd really hoped we'd see one," I told the keeper, hopelessly.

It didn't take a genius to read Kate's body language at that point. She was crushed.

"I understand," the keeper said, "They're an interesting bird. We're cleaning up here. I've been told there's a zoo up north that's willing to part with a breeding pair, so we're trying to make that happen."

"Do you know when?"

"Sorry, I'm not sure. It may not be for a while. And before that happens, I still need to work out what needs fixing here. Still haven't found where the damn snake got in."

"Ok, thanks anyway."

I swear it was as if the world was conspiring against her. It's easy to admit that the rest of the zoo held little appeal after that. The day never recovered and the rest of the exhibits slipped by barely noticed. Kate was a lot more subdued the rest of the day and I didn't know what to say. Couldn't I do anything right by her? I knew it wasn't my fault, but that didn't change things. What could *I* do to make her happier? At that moment, I was beginning to feel like the answer was that there wasn't anything I could do.

Mum picked us up shortly after. She didn't ask questions when Kate asked that she be dropped off a few houses down from her place after a quiet car ride. I'm sure she could tell things weren't right. Mum waited in the car as I walked with her the short distance to her place.

"Are you going to be able to get back inside without your Dad noticing?" I asked as we ducked down out of sight.

She nodded without a word.

"I'm sorry about today; I had hoped it would be more enjoyable than that."

"Don't worry about today," she said with a smile that didn't quite find happiness. "There will be a next time."

She looked at me intently. "Hey. I mean it. It wasn't your fault. Now watch closely. He won't notice a thing."

She slipped in silently through her front gate, clearly holding some experience at opening the rusty latch without a sound. Her movements across her front lawn were well-practiced as she stole across the yard between the car bodies and open front windows to end crouched under a small side window. With deft hands, she lifted the window high enough to slip herself in, sliding headfirst into the window. She hung her head out the window and flashed me a thumbs up. Then she disappeared, mischief achieved.

There was a loud voice, a loud thump, then nothing more.

Friday Afternoon December 19th 1997

The afternoon started with a slice of a new Mexican-themed pizza that my boss was experimenting with. It needed work. A lot of it. However, it provided all the major food groups a teenager needed, pizza dough, some slices of meat approximate, random green things and plenty of dairy melted over the top. Zach and I had gone for lunch, but, at least for me, things felt wrong without Lizzie. It wasn't the same being in there eating pizza without the three of us together. But, I guess that's the way things go.

"You know, Lizzie has been looking for you," I told Zach. "She came to me the other night at the party asking where you were. Must have seen you."

"With Erin?"

"Maybe. Don't think so. She didn't say anything. Speaking of which…"

"Don't say it."

"It's just, don't you think…"

"I said, don't say it."

I ignored him.

"But don't you think it was a little soon?"

"Look, haven't you been paying attention to anything I've been saying lately? Here's the deal. I'm only going to say this once so listen carefully. These whole rules that our society has developed around all this dating and relationship stuff, it's all complete bullshit. This whole, you have to wait this long before you do this, or you can't do this without doing that. All complete bullshit. You and Kate? Be pragmatic. If you want to do something, if she wants to do something, you do it. If you don't, or she doesn't, you both don't, you don't. Whether one year feels right or one day does. Whatever works, works. Don't judge, you have to be cool with people's choices."

"I'm not judging, it seemed rather quick, that's all."

"It worked," he said with a shrug, and then, after a short delay, a wink. "I hope you're not expecting details here, a man doesn't kiss and tell."

"And since when were you a man?"

"Ouch. That hurts." He took a bite of pizza, shook his head in thought for a moment and then said, "She was fucking hot man, like, oh boy."

"What happened to not kissing and telling?"

"All I'm saying is… she knew exactly what she wanted."

"And what was that?"

He shrugged and grinned from ear to ear.

"Enough said."

"No, not enough said," he said with a laugh. "You don't think sneaking off with Kate on that couch went unnoticed do you. Well?"

"Well what?"

"What about you and Kate?"

"I don't know, it's weird man."

"There's nothing weird about those, Sam. Some are bigger like Kate's, some are smaller like Erin's, but they're all good. Trust me, there's nothing weird there."

Trust him to go there. I couldn't help a short laugh. "That is not even remotely close to what I mean. There's something weird about her."

"Oh, all girls are a little weird. A little crazy. A little crazy is good. Too much crazy isn't so good, but a little isn't so bad. Erin was a little crazy once we got into, well, you know what I mean."

"Too much information and no, no, no, you're not listening. It's more than that. She's hiding something."

He laughed at me. "They're all hiding something Sam. Everybody keeps secrets. Don't worry about it. She's fine. She doesn't come across as crazy crazy so there's nothing to worry about. I get it. You're new to this so you're confused and stuff. Relax and don't invent issues that don't exist. You have an amazing thing going for you. So don't go crazy crazy on her. Stick to plain old crazy."

"You think?"

"I know. Relax. Eat more pizza too. I don't remember it being this hard to get through it all."

"Have you thought about what you're going to get Erin for Christmas?" I asked.

"Shit."

"I know, right."

"What the fuck am I supposed to do there? How the fuck should I know what to get her?"

"How ironic."

He rolled his eyes at me.

"Well, what are you doing after lunch?" I asked. "Feel like helping me shop for Kate's present?" I asked with a mouth half-full pizza.

"Shopping? Seriously? Maybe it is too late for you. Shopping! Sounds like you're already crazy crazy."

"And how the hell are you going to get her a gift if you don't go shopping?"

"You raise a good point. However, as much as I'd love to brave the crazies in the Christmas shopping crowds, I'm afraid this afternoon I get the pleasure of dealing with them from behind the counter at work."

"Sounds like fun."

"You have no idea."

Seriously, how the hell does anybody understand what's going on with all these different camera lens models? There are so many different numbers. Even with the model number for Kate's broken lens in hand, I had no idea where to begin. Well, except for the fact that I could discount purchasing 99% of the models on price alone. How could they be worth so much, they're a couple of glass lenses and a bit of plastic, right?

The sales people circled, having smelled blood in the water. I handed over my sheet of paper to the nearest one with the model number of Kate's broken lens on it. It was the best I felt I could do to placate the sharks without making it blindingly obvious I was out of my depth. I hope I at least managed that. I avoided all eye contact, just in case.

He looked disappointed as he pointed me toward the right lens. It was 'on special', from $200 to $190. 'On special' my arse. I asked if there was anything cheaper that would still work in the same camera. He scoffed at me. Didn't actually answer the question mind you, but that was enough to tell me all I needed to know. I died a little inside. Zach would have called it stupid, a poor investment, but no matter how much it hurt my bank account, it was still something I had set myself to do. It was as simple as that, nothing was worth as much as seeing her happy again. It would be worth it, I told myself, I knew it.

It meant the gifts I got for my family were a little on the light side. It didn't take long for the crowds to start overwhelming me. Too much noise. Too many unwashed crazies. The place was absolute chaos. I didn't realise this town had that many people. The shopping centre was bursting at the seams. So was my head, as my brain went into introversion meltdown. Getting out was a relief.

Sorcha greeted me at the gate with her usual enthusiasm, though her exuberance turned quickly forlorn when I, with hands full of shopping bags, wasn't able to give her an expected scratch. Giving up, she rushed past me inside.

"What do you have there?" Kate asked.

There was only one time I wasn't happy to hear that voice, and it was then. With my hands full, there was no chance of hiding the shopping bag holding her Christmas gift, quite obviously marked with the camera store's logo. I'd almost come to expect that sort of horrible timing.

Sorcha almost came to my rescue. A small part of me believed it was even intentional to save me. At least I wanted to believe. She mistook Kate's exuberance to see me as eagerness to give attention and jumped up into her arms. The moment's distraction seemed fortuitous; it was long enough for me to throw the bag out of sight into a pile of clothes left in the laundry nearby.

"Oh nothing much, some Christmas gifts for my family," I responded.

"Anything for me?" She craned her neck to try to see around me.

I came so close to getting away with it. The time to respond with some convincing lie flashed past before my stupefied self even considered it an option. I needed to work on being a better liar. Or perhaps being a better liar to my girlfriend wasn't such a good thing? To this day, I'm still unsure of the answer to that question.

"So, anyway, what are you doing for Christmas?" Dodging the question wasn't lying, was it?

She flashed me a look of mild disapproval. Sorcha took that as permission to lick her face.

"Geez, thanks." Kate laughed at Sorcha. "Lying by omission is still lying Sam, and you're a shitty liar. Come on, tell me what you got."

I admitted that it was her Christmas present and I wasn't ready to show her yet. So much for that secret.

"You shouldn't have gotten me any... oh... -thing,"

Her words trailed off as my miserable attempt at hiding the camera store shopping bag failed.

"Is that what I think it is?"

"I hadn't…"

"Is that what I think it is?" she asked again, her eyes fixated on me excitedly begging me to answer her question.

"I had hoped to keep it as a secret until Christmas, you know."

Nothing ever went to plan with Kate. It took me too long to realise the appeal in that.

"I guess I hadn't thought much about Christmas," she said. "Did you have something planned?"

"Oh, I was wondering if you wanted to have Christmas lunch with us? We always have a big family thing. If you're not doing anything else."

"Is that ok with your parents?"

"It should be."

"You don't know?"

"I don't see why it would be a problem. Why would it be?"

"My family doesn't really do Christmas. Not like big Christmas dinners or anything like. I wouldn't want to intrude or anything."

"You wouldn't be."

"You sure?"

"Yes I'm sure."

"Why are you looking at me funny?"

What was that about lying? Oh yes, respond quickly.

"What, I'm not."

"You're a shitty liar Sam."

Perhaps it needed a touch more assertiveness.

"So ah, how come you're around here?"

"Haven't we gone through this before? I'm your girlfriend and I'll come around to see my boyfriend whenever I damn well please. Also, did you forget? Friday night is date night."

"But aren't you grounded?"

"Yeah, and?"

"Did your father catch you the other day? Because I got the impression as I left that he wasn't particularly happy."

"Yeah well…" Her vivacity slipped a moment too long. What was it that I had said about lying?

"Oh, don't worry about it. I suppose, technically speaking, I'm still grounded. Fuck him though, you know? Actually, I also… anyways, don't worry about that."

The liar's dance continued. I picked up the shopping bag and handed it to her.

"So yeah, I got you this."

"Are you sure you want me to open it? If you had plans for Christmas…"

"No, now is good."

One final turn around the floor.

She pounced on the bag, like a young kid on Christmas. Next came the squealing, because the young kid hit the jackpot at Christmas. Even mother called out from upstairs to ask if everything was ok.

The cost of that gift was completely worth it, if only for those moments of unadulterated bliss. No regrets.

She turned the box over in her hands, checking out all the details closely.

"I can't believe you got me this, how did you afford it?"

I just shrugged. She just smothered me with kisses. A fair trade, in my opinion.

A short kiss became a series of much longer kisses, a door became closed, dinners skipped, hands became occupied and the date night became a lost cause.

It couldn't last, naturally. My own insecurities were a constant, of course, but the more they bubbled to the surface, the more they demanded attention. And right then, they were demanding attention, naturally choosing the most awkward of times. I knew the unanswered questions would keep swirling around in my head until they consumed me. And the answers needed to come, no matter how much I knew I shouldn't ask. Or how stupid I looked. It's only stupid self-destruction.

"Why me?" The question slipped out before I could stop it.

She looked at me confused for a moment then gently shook her head.

"Haven't we been through this?"

"But it doesn't make sense. Why would you, the most beautiful girl ever, ever want to date some unattractive, introverted nobody with zero relationship experience? Why?"

"Because maybe I'm not the most beautiful girl ever. Because maybe if I wanted somebody with more relationship experience I would have left you ages ago. Which is saying something considering we haven't been going out that long. Because maybe I like that you're an introvert and I like how much you think about things. But also because maybe you think too much and need to do a bit more feeling. Because maybe being with you makes me stop thinking so much and feel a whole lot more. Maybe that makes me crazy but I'll take this crazy any day."

"Definitely crazy."

She laughed as she looked out the window. There wasn't much to see, it was late, already dark.

"Well, I'm definitely crazy for staying out this late. Date night or not, you're not wrong about my father. Sorry boy, time for me to bail," she said as she slid off me and clipped up her bra.

"Wait, what's up with your father, why's he so mad at you anyway?"

Kate paused to lean against the doorframe, her hand finding her hip. She looked back over her shoulder, melancholic.

"Be careful of the stones you turn over, Sam, you might not like what's lurking underneath."

I almost audibly sighed. Why did she have to go and say something like that?

"Oh, I almost forgot, I did have another reason for coming around. You distracted me. I came around to ask you what you were doing for New Year's."

"New Year's? I hadn't even thought about it."

"How could you not have thought about New Year's?" She laughed briefly. "Never mind, I think I'm beginning to understand. There's a plan forming. The three of us were talking about going camping over New Year's. By ourselves, and you guys of course, because fuck other people. That and Amy won't come if it's a huge thing. They were talking about heading to a beach up north, but I've been thinking about our lyrebird quest and I think I want to make that happen. There are camping grounds south that cross into real lyrebird territory and I think we could make these photos happen. Not that I told them the truth, I'm sure they wouldn't understand, but I was able to convince them. Erin was keen. I assume that will be enough to draw Zach's interest. Even Amy seemed keen, in her own way. Interested?"

Wednesday Afternoon December 25th 1997

"I think I'm going to head home," Kate said to me quietly away from the rest of my family.

Christmas lunch activities had started to die down. Three families crammed into whatever shade they were able to find around the back of our house. Christmas that year was as ridiculously hot as any other, and everyone was slowly slipping into a well-sated food coma from having eaten too much Christmas lunch. Dad snored away in a folding camp chair, having already succumbed. Mum was discussing one of my cousins' upcoming wedding with my aunts, while a cabal of screaming kids ran around the backyard, ignored by everyone except Sorcha, who bounded after them.

"Why?" I asked.

"You have a really happy family."

I had no idea what that had to do with anything.

"I don't belong here."

"I don't understand."

"You don't need to. Just old memories. Tell your mum thanks for the lunch. The food was really good."

I held her wrist and asked her to stay. She kissed me on the cheek, shook her head and walked out.

Mum walked up to me not long after.

"Where did Kate go?

"She had some family thing to get back to. Some family dinner or something."

"Oh, ok. Well, next time you see her, tell her to write down the recipe to that potato bake she brought. It was amazing."

Yeah Mum. Of all the things I felt I needed to ask Kate about, potato bake was the last thing I had in mind.

Wednesday Afternoon December 31st 1997

"So whose smart idea was it to let Kate drive again?" Amy said from the back of Kate's ridiculously overloaded car as it bounced down the dirt road to the camping grounds. We were in the middle of nowhere, driving down a forgotten road deep in the blue mountains on our way to an allegedly awesome campground – Kate's words. To make things even more fun, a light downfall that morning had turned the dirt road into slick mud, we were already running late and Kate wasn't ever shy driving beyond the limit.

"You're lucky," Kate said. "If you were anybody else I'd kick you out of the car right now."

"So, whose idea was it to let you drive?" I quipped.

Kate hit the brakes. The car skidded to a halt, sliding sideways until it stopped inches from a tree jutting out at the edge of the road. We sat there, unmoving, as Kate sat grumbling, conflicted with whom she was the least impressed.

"Remember what happened with the last car you had Kate?" Amy poked.

"Oh shut up! It's not like either of you can drive. You can both bloody walk for all I care," Kate grumbled, struggling to hold back laughter.

A wave of dirt covered Kate car as Erin's car flew past us.

"Oh hell no," Kate yelled as she floored the car. It fishtailed down the road as she struggled to keep the steering centred on the loose road.

"I'll take that as a no," Amy remarked.

All we could do was hold on for dear life as Kate rocketed the car down the rough bush track. To this day, I have no idea how she managed to overtake Erin on that narrow dirt road but somehow, by the time Erin and Zach arrived at the camping grounds, we had been waiting for at least five minutes.

At the end of the road, the dense forest opened out into a small field. In the middle were the burnt-out remains of previous camping fires and off to the side was a less than appealing toilet block with an even less appealing tap hanging off the side. The field sloped down to a river that casually wound past the campground, widened to about ten metres at the point it passed the campsite, before it turned a sharp corner and flowed off into the distance. Apart from us, the camping grounds were empty.

Although the rain had lightened to a drizzle, it caused us all sorts of havoc, having turned the field into a damp, muddy mess. We threw the parts to our three dome tents haphazardly on the ground while we searched out the driest part of the field to set up the tents. We settled for a spot near the centre next to an old fire pit and set the tents up as quickly as possible in the continuing rain. As is so common in such situations, the faster we needed to be, the slower we succeeded in being. Stick three poles together and attach them to the clips on the tent, hammer in some pegs, how hard could it be, right? Kate, at least, had an excuse, because while she'd upgraded from a cast to a brace, she still wasn't supposed to do anything strenuous. But if Kate and I were doing poorly, Erin and Zach were really struggling. Zach had finally gotten three of the four corner tent pegs driven into the ground, after a three-minute debate between them as to the best place to pitch the tent, and a follow up two minute debate when that chosen site turned out to be a mushy mess. Erin had just finished sliding the second tent pole through the tent's loops when she realised that she'd used the wrong length of pole. She threw her arms up in frustration and stormed away.

"That's because that pole doesn't go in there," Amy pointed out dispassionately.

"That's what I tried to say," I added.

"No shit! If you two know so much, why don't you put the bloody thing up?" Erin sat down with a huff in her camp chair.

We had it finished five minutes later. Turns out, not having anybody to argue with speeds up the process of putting up a tent. Erin stewed the whole time, looking miserable as the rain continued to soak her.

"Don't say it," Erin growled.

Zach turned and shrugged at us. Which was a terrible decision to make. She saw it and slumped lower in her chair. Kate rushed in to try to diffuse the situation, grabbing a can of vodka premix from one of the coolers and throwing it at her.

"Here you go grumpy face."

Erin took it without responding. Kate mouthed 'oh dear' to the rest of us. The heavens chose that moment to give us one final drenching, which really drove home the miserable situation. And, as if to taunt us, it stopped almost as soon as we'd finished putting everything together.

"Now what?" I asked.

"Burn all the things." Amy said in a serious monotone.

"Say what?" Kate asked, as shocked as I was by her random comment.

"Amy, you know, you can be really weird sometimes," Zach added. "Just saying…"

"All I meant was, starting a fire wouldn't hurt," Amy bit back. "You know, cook some dinner or something."

"It's a little early, isn't it," Zach said.

Amy rolled her eyes up to the sky.

"While it's stopped raining," she added, forcefully.

"Right… good idea," Zach said. He pointed to the cooler. "Perhaps a few more of those would help things."

As Kate handed out drinks, Amy set to starting a fire. I immediately offered to help Amy with the fire, but she glared at me so hard I didn't say another word. Being an ex-scout had taught me to be prepared, and I'd come prepared with enough fire starting paraphernalia to start a fire in the worst conditions. But she seemed determined to do things her own way and with that glare, I was too scared to say a word against her.

However, it became quickly apparent by the way she was going about it that she wasn't going to be starting that fire any time soon. The dampness added to the difficulty and I'm sure it didn't help that the rest of us sat there staring stupidly at her as she grew more and more frustrated. She got a further five minutes of my patience before I caved to the frustration.

"Here, can I help?" I asked tentatively as I knelt down beside the fire.

But there's no subtle way to take over from somebody so determined but failing. At least, not in any way that doesn't make them feel inadequate. Amy's eyes could have started the fire then and there the way they burnt through me.

From my kit, I took some cotton wool that I'd dipped in Vaseline, an assortment of flammable liquids and other stuff that you won't find in any official guide and would probably get me in trouble were I to start being specific. I rearranged the firewood to allow more oxygen in, added the cotton wool, some tinder, liberally applied some of the other substances and, with a few strikes of a magnesium flint, almost set myself on fire. The pile of timber went up in flame very quickly. Of course, it's one thing to start a fire, keeping it burning takes more than just a few bright sparks.

And it's one thing to keep a fire burning and completely another to use it to turn out edible food. The charred sausages didn't bother me so much, but the others barred me from any further cooking for the trip. Unsurprisingly, that didn't bother me.

It was clear to everyone that the trip had started poorly. The conversation was jilted and tense as we sat around the fire burning the afternoon. Something had to break eventually. In what was perhaps a measure of the strength of our five wills, nature flinched first. And by flinch, I mean it started bucketing down again. I really expected that this torrent would be the straw that broke us. We sat in our chairs and took the rain as it came. Nobody moved. I think all of us were so over it by that stage that nobody bothered trying to stay dry. Looking around, everyone was soaked, miserable and defeated.

Then Kate laughed. It started as soft rumble but it was soon outright hysterical, manic laughter. She jumped out of her chair so quickly it fell backwards. Still laughing away to herself, she stood in the rain and stripped off her wet shirt and pants.

"Oh shit, Kate's finally lost it," Amy exclaimed.

Down to nothing but her bra and briefs, Kate ran for the river, kicking her shoes off on the way before hitting the water at full speed. Taking a second to rip off her wrist brace and throw it at the shore, she waded in up to her thighs, turned to face us and raised both arms up to the sky.

"Fuck you, Fate!" she yelled as she proceeded to flip off the sky. Then, with a flourish, she tumbled backwards into the water, creating a massive splash.

Once the water had settled, Kate surfaced on her back, floating on the river and completely relaxed. Her entire sequence was to this day the most amazing thing I had ever witnessed. It also represented the turning point for the rest of the trip. Perhaps overawed by the sheer audacity or insanity – your choice – the tension slipped from the afternoon like the rain slipped down Kate's less than naked body. Sure, it may have still been there but nobody cared anymore.

Erin quickly took up the cause. Following Kate's lead, she ran toward the river, laughing the entire way. She hit the water running and she kept going until she was underwater. Her head bobbed up moments later close to Kate. Zach followed her close behind, only a blur across my vision as my attention had been on Erin's entry. Zach leapt from the shore, unceremoniously belly flopping into the river and covering them both with a giant wave of water.

That left Amy and I, the least free spirited, still above water. Kate lifted her head momentarily to stare directly at me. No words necessary, the look said everything and not one to resist peer pressure, I soon found myself half-naked, hip deep and heading deeper. Despite it being summer, the water was crisp enough to make me think twice about what I was doing, enough to make me flinch at completely submersing myself. And, although the flowing water looked crystal clean, the riverbed was a disgusting, silty sticky mud that seemed like it was trying to suck you in. I was waist deep when, to my amazement, and the others' as well, judging by their expressions, Amy walked in beside me, smirking as she measured their surprised faces. She took another step past me, then somehow, in a way I feel only she could, found an elegant way to fall face first into the water. It wasn't a dive so much; she just slid forward and the water embraced her. Either way, it was beyond my grace to repeat.

Kate slid behind me, wrapped a dripping wet arm across my collar and planted a hint of seduction on the back of my neck. I had started to sink into the comfortable feeling of her embrace when she pushed my knees out from under me with her own and forced me backwards into the water. The sudden rush of murky coldness was particularly unpleasant. I came up spluttering.

"What?" Kate asked playfully.

The spray of water she got in return was well earned though I certainly don't think I deserved the spray she responded with. Apparently, Erin wasn't particularly thrilled about being sprayed with water either, so she started shoving water at both of us. That opened hostilities for everyone and that small bend in the river turned into a storm of water and laughter, all teenage passion thrown into the pursuit of our happiness.

Things lasted until we were exhausted, which, given my level of fitness, wasn't very long but, given my level of fitness, long enough. We five sat around, spent, with only our heads bobbing in a circle above the black glaze as the last light left us. A mischievous grin grew across Erin's face; the first outward reflection of a sly plan she'd been hatching. A ripple of water belied action. A lip bitten in consideration pursed as she came to a decision. She lifted her right hand clenched above the water and, as we all realised she held what remained of her clothes, shocked us all by throwing them toward the shore. From that point, the only thing hiding her modesty was the physics of light refraction through rippling water. Not that she seemed concerned.

"Well, are you all chicken?" she said, holding her hands up coquettishly.

Kate looked curious. Amy looked horrified. And Zach? He looked closer.

Kate shuffled under the water.

"Eyes up, mister," she said when she noticed me looking in her direction.

Her underwear joined Erin's on the river's bank. Zach gave a quick shrug, a giant grin and flung his as well. Amy held out, her eyes closed with her head shaking in denial. Kate gave her a playful shove. She let one final sigh, mumbled something to herself then threw her clothes away as well. I honestly expected more resistance from her.

That left me. All eyes turned my way. I had a hard time meeting them and a harder time not looking elsewhere.

"Sam Price you will remove your clothes immediately or there will be hell to pay," Kate said.

What was that I'd said previously about peer pressure? It joined the rest on the riverbank.

"Good, that's sorted," Erin said.

It was dark, exceptionally dark. Though the clouds had started to break up, the moon had decided to take the day off. Even the tiny ripples caused by the last of the light rainfall couldn't hide the diverse tints of flesh that swirled under the surface of the black water. Our interaction was a strange dichotomy of nervous laughter and sexual tension, nothing actually happened and yet everything was happening.

Now it may seem like this was a good start into a teenage boy's fantasy, and for a moment there it was, but with the sun long since set things got cold very quickly. Cue jokes about shrinkage. And that left us in an awkward situation. So far, everything had been flashes and hints of flesh. We all started to shiver. Kate seemed to be the worst affected, her lips had started to turn blue. That was a conundrum in itself. Was I supposed to try to warm her up somehow? I wasn't quite sure where I stood with the questions that raised.

"Be a good boyfriend and go get me a towel," Erin said to Zach between chattering teeth.

"Why don't you be a good girlfriend and go get me one?" he retorted.

I'm certain it was only the blithe hope he wove into that playful remark that kept him alive that moment. I think, given earlier events, he probably should have reconsidered saying it. He hesitated, mentally preparing himself.

Amy threw another heavy sigh.

"You are all so immature," she said and then started walking out. She left the water as gracefully as she entered it.

With her black hair clinging to her pale back facing toward us, she covered what she could with her two arms. She wasn't entirely successful. A quick glance to the others showed they were paying as much attention as I was. Kate caught my eye. Then she hit me across the shoulder.

"You're not supposed to look."

"You're looking."

"I can't help it, she's beautiful."

"I know."

I regretted it as soon as I said it. I could have died right then and not felt worse in my life. So I waited like a condemned man on his last day waiting for the axe to fall. It never did.

"You know, after saying something like that, you're supposed to tell me how you think I'm more beautiful," she poked. I'm not sure if she didn't read into it the same way I did, or she let me off the hook that day. In some way, like the condemned man, not knowing was more agony.

Zach must have worked up enough courage by this point, because the moment Amy kneeled down to pick up her clothes, still artfully covered, he came streaking out of the water in a burst of water. It was about as opposite of Amy's graceful exit as one could be. I saw far more of my friend in that moment than I cared for. Amy took one look at him, screeched in surprise and lost it. That was her mistake. While Zach had committed to running through the wet and slippery ground, taking each step confidently, she hadn't. As she went to bolt, her left foot lost traction sending her face down into the mud. Grace abandoned. Chaos. And the more she panicked the more the mud conspired against her. Her one saving grace was that the night was so dark that the finer details were lost to the night. Once she'd found her feet, she ran for her tent. Coming out moments later with a towel wrapped loosely around herself, she bolted, head down, straight for the shower block.

Zach, on the other hand, took his time. I don't suspect I'll ever be able to scrub the sight of him completely naked from my mind as he disappeared into his tent. Once wrapped in his own towel, he then disappeared into Kate's and my tent. After what seemed like an excessive amount of time, he finally came out, taking his sweet time coming back to the water's edge with towels for each of us. I could see what was about to happen. He made it out until the water was at his knees before realisation hit him. The water started lapping at the towel wrapped around him. And even leaning out as far as he could, he was still not quite within reach.

"You idiot," I said.

I'd barely gotten the words out when my towel hit me in the face. Once he'd thrown the rest of the towels out to everyone else, we all, holding our towels awkwardly above our heads, took to consider the logistics of how to get the towels around us, keep them dry and not expose anything that we didn't desire to. The girls had a harder time of it than I did, but with some quick hands and careful timing, they managed to avoid anything too embarrassing. I wasn't so lucky. Let this be said about towels; they might absorb water well enough when you need them to but they're useless at hiding certain male physical reactions. It didn't slip Kate's notice. I waited for the inevitable joke but it never came. Instead, her bitten lip helped my cheeks discover some of the last remaining warmth from deep inside me.

The next few minutes weren't any less awkward. First, I was stuck outside our tent, still in nothing but this towel because despite the afternoon's activities Kate wasn't comfortable with me being in there while she changed. Fair enough, I guess, but Zach and Erin didn't bear the same objections. It would probably seem like a good thing considering I was desperately trying to will the undesired forth tent to un-pitch itself were it not for the second, as I caught Amy trying to slip unnoticed into the camp. She must not have seen me, but recognition was clear as our eyes crossed. So how do you come back from, I've seen you naked and don't mind my erection? Where do you go from there? We stood frozen, locked in uncertainty for who knows how long. To move would be to admit the uncomfortable reality, and neither of us could. And all I wanted to know? What she was thinking?

The sound of a zipper tore us apart. It had happened within a fraction of a second, a moment spawning a lifetime of questions that I would never know the answers to. Kate stepped out of the tent. Amy was already gone.

"All yours."

As a side point, I discovered why Zach had taken so long in our tent and I'm glad that it appeared Kate didn't. Inserted into the top of my bag was a brief and hastily written note with just the word 'Enjoy' written on it, wrapped with a rubber band around a packet of condoms. It felt a little presumptuous, although I did consider that I should be thankful that at least he'd been discreet about it. Knowing him, it could have gone completely differently. I tucked them deep out of sight.

"I can't believe nobody remembered to bring a fucking watch," Kate said laughing. "How the fuck are we supposed to tell it's midnight if we don't know what the fucking time is?"

Everybody looked at her sheepishly. She had a point. We sat on our chairs staring into fire, heads spinning from the alcohol and doing our best not to bring up the events of the afternoon. Kate sat close, her head tucked gently against my neck. Zach and Erin, off in their own world, seemed to be ignorant to us being able see everything they were up to. Amy, the only one of us not actually sitting, was flat on her back staring at the sky. She seemed trying especially hard not to remember anything judging by the number of empty drink cans that lay haphazardly beside her. I also suspected that at that point she couldn't actually sit. She was mumbling vaguely about the apparent sexism in Disney movies, a conversation topic that, to my best judgement, had wrapped up at least an hour previous.

And I watched Kate intently. Her hair glowed in the ambiance of fire; her face vexed with unspoken thoughts. I was perplexed that she hadn't had much to drink. It didn't seem like her. She'd be acting a little odd lately, since Christmas, but nothing I could put my finger on. As distant as the stars. If only I could have said so, to tell her as I saw her, so bright as to mock the stars themselves.

"Why don't we call midnight and be done with it?" Zach said hastily between Erin's lips. "I mean, it's got to be midnight somewhere, right?"

"I guess so," I responded

"So happy new years and everything, woohoo and shit, we're going to bed," he rushed as they both stood up. They didn't even bother waiting for any response before they hurried off into their tent. I rolled my eyes and shrugged at Kate.

"Oh, let them have their fun."

"They could have, you know…"

"Made it less obvious? I'm not so sure they could have. Come on, we should follow their lead," she said as she nuzzled her cheek against my shoulder.

Beside us, Amy gurgled out something vaguely along the lines of 'happy new year', groaned and curled herself up into a ball. We both shared a laugh.

"Do you think we should help her into her tent?" I asked.

Kate pondered Amy for a moment. "Probably."

She reached down and tried lifting Amy up by her arm. Amy groaned loudly and waved her off.

"Come on, up you get," Kate said.

Amy mumbled something that sounded like 'go away'.

"Do you think it's ok to leave her out here?" I asked

Kate nodded. "I think she'll be ok. I guess once some of the alcohol wears off, she can find her own way to her tent."

Kate slipped inside our tent. Something didn't feel right, leaving Amy outside like that. I took a blanket from the car and tried to wrap her up as warmly as she would allow. Kate, her head stuck outside the entrance of the tent, nodded approvingly.

"She's going to regret it in the morning," I said.

That elicited a small grin. "She's going to regret a lot of things in the morning. Come on."

I crawled into the tent to find Kate kneeling in the middle of the tent, facing the entrance. She held her hand out and pulled mine close. Her eyes looked out at me from the mask she wore and I swear I thought she was about to cry. I opened my mouth to ask.

"I know that look, don't you start. It's nothing, I promise. Don't worry; it's just thoughts about the old year. I just want this year to be different."

"What can I do to make it better?"

"You already are." A deep sigh seemed to release her thoughts. A change flickered across her face; a devious smile peaked out from under the mask. We sat in the dark, kneeling with our knees touching and our faces inches apart. She leant closer until her lips hovered next to my ear. I want to say that I reacted in some suave manner but secretly I was shitting myself, uncertain what to expect.

"Tell me something Sam, have you ever touched a girl before?"

"I've touched you."

Her hands were holding mine.

"No, I don't mean like that, I mean like this…"

Pubic hair is a strange thing. I had seen, in my formative teenage years, pictures demonstrating all manner of ways of presenting it, yet it was her unkempt tangle my fingers soon found that held the most allure. Her brown hair fell over my face in her ecstasy. Then she pushed me down. And so, that's how that night I reached third base with Kate. And vice versa. But that's enough gory details. Though since I'm sure you're wondering, no, I never came to need the 'gifts' Zach gave me. They remained safely tucked deep within my bag. And I wasn't the least bit unhappy with this.

Thursday Morning January 1st 1998

Difficult was waking up next to the naked form of the most beautiful girl I'd ever known and resisting the urge to reach out and touch her, knowing that that would be to destroy the beauty in the observed, and every other sense screamed to share the sight. I held a million curiosities and she was all of them. I loved the way her skin was so pale I could almost see the heart beat in each blush of her cheek. I loved the way the curve of her hips met her ribs. I loved the way her body curved away from me and I loved how her arm curled under the curves of her breasts. I loved the dip her spine made in her back and how her sable hair fell on the floor between us. Oh how I loved all the shades of her hair, each strand unique and I loved more that I had the opportunity to observe them all.

And I hated that what words I had to tell her beauty were so woefully inadequate and I hated how they would never be adequate. Mostly, I hated the fear that if I reached out to hold her, the naïve want to stop her from slipping away, that beautiful moment would slip away and I'd never experience anything so beautiful again. The fear was already pulling that moment away. I had to leave before the only memory I had was the fear there was nothing I could do.

Outside, the first breath of air bit back. The sun hovered above the horizon but hadn't quite broken the tree line. The ground was wet with dew, the fire spent ash and, surprisingly, a prone bundle of blankets hinted Amy still lay curled up next it. Part of me was impressed she lasted the night out here.

I made a rash decision not to bother with shoes on the trip to the toilet block. It was a decision I regretted almost immediately. The ground was icy cold, which made no sense to me given it was the middle of summer. Yet this little glade in the forest was freezing. You know that pain you get when your ankles are so cold and frozen the muscles cramp and send stabbing pains through your shins and yet nobody ever seems to know why it happens? It was a whole lot of that. Then, once that pain had finally abated, the realisation that I had stumbled into a massive bindi patch kicked in, and that it was only the icy cold ground that had numbed my feet and stopped me from noticing the sharp needle-like thorns jabbing into the soles of my feet. By that point, I was far too committed and it was closer to keep walking than to turn back. It is the great Australian nightmare, wandering into a patch of nature's little caltrops with no idea how far the patch spreads out.

The reward for picking out 32 (I counted) of the damn things was four walls of cold concrete and a colder shower. Leaving a warm tent and a beautiful naked woman to walk through a painful bindi patch to have a shower was the perfect summation of how I seemed to approach my life until that point. It was one big painful mistake.

The shower was worse than you'd imagine. No, not the bad you're imagining, worse. The kind of worse that lifetime regrets are made of. And after it, I had the return trip back through the bindi patch to steel myself for, to get back to the warm sleeping bag and her. There's no metaphor there, only twenty metres of pain and suffering.

Pulling out the seventeenth bindi (I wasn't actually counting. The number is a complete fabrication and I didn't give a shit at that point beyond wanting to get the damn things out) woke Amy. So many times, I would have said Amy could never not look attractive. This wasn't one of those times. Her especially pale face, with half-cocked eyes and a tangle of hair covering her face poked out from under her blanket.

"Shit," she groaned as she sat up and took in her surroundings.

It seemed an appropriate measure of how she looked and no doubt felt.

"Why did you leave me out here?" she asked me.

"We tried moving you. You were pretty set on staying where you are."

"I don't remember that part of the night."

"That's not surprising. You drank an awful lot. Can I get you anything?"

She made an effort of getting up, but waved me off. Eyes wide open, lips sealed shut. She aimed for her tent, stumbling toward it. She bounced off the entrance, half spun away but too quickly given her current state, made it an impressive six steps toward the trees behind her tent, landed on her knees and projectile vomited a night's worth of regret out. It was oddly ungraceful. I grabbed a nearby bottle of water, sat with her, holding her hair out of the way and rubbing her back gently. I didn't know what else to do.

She tried to push me away between heaves.

"Please go away. I'm fine," she slurred.

Hardly. I left the bottle of water at her side and gave her arm one final assuring pat. I turned to find Kate watching us. She was wearing a mix of panic and concern and though she was looking directly at me, I figured it was directed at Amy. It slipped away as soon as she realised I was looking at her. I wondered what she'd just assumed. Or was I imagining things?

It could have been the early morning sun blinding her. I hoped. We slowly closed the distance between us. She seemed unsteady. I noticed a slight hesitation before she stepped up close to me. I think I noticed it. I probably imagined it. She leaned in and kissed me on the cheek.

"Morning. How is she?" Kate asked.

"About what you'd expect."

"Do you think she'll be ok?"

"I think she'll survive."

"I've never seen her drink that much. Hell, I don't think I've ever seen her drink close to that much before."

"She seemed a little embarrassed last night."

"Yesterday wasn't like her at all."

Zach and Erin chose that moment to look at what was going on outside their tent. It was comical the way their heads peeked out almost simultaneously, one above the other, with opposing eyes, Zach right, Erin left, squinting in the sudden light. They took in us first, then Amy, shook their heads in mock disapproval then disappeared again.

"And then there's those two," I said.

Kate chuckled while guiding me back to our tent.

"Don't go anywhere, I'll be back shortly," she said as she turned and rapidly walked toward the showers.

"Put some shoes on, trust me!" I yelled out to her.

She gave me a vacant look, shrugged and kept walking. It was painful watching her.

"I'm sorry," Kate half whispered, giggling with embarrassment. "I was a little loud, wasn't I?"

"A little bit."

"Take it as a compliment." She sighed and nuzzled her chin into my neck. "We should, I don't know, probably do something. Like, as much as I wouldn't mind spending all day in this tent going over that again, I had planned on taking my camera out for some bird hunting."

"I'm up for some of that."

She sat back, considering me and then nodded in agreement.

"I'm going to need another shower. With shoes this time."

"I did try and tell you."

"I know, and stupid me didn't listen."

"I also think you're crazy wanting to take another freezing shower."

"Yeah well, thanks to you it's a necessity."

She kissed me briefly. Long enough to get me to stop me asking more questions, I suspect. Watching her put on her pants was easily as sexy as watching her take them off, despite her struggle within the confines of this tent.

"Shall we?" She pointed to the tent entrance with her eyes.

I may not have been telling the entire truth about being happy to go do other activities. Well, let's be honest, outside was the last place I wanted to be. I also didn't enjoy the heat my cheeks gave off as they all unashamedly stared at us as we stepped outside. Amy, green as she was, tried to look like she wasn't looking and in doing so only managed to give away how closely she was looking. Erin didn't hide her attention, pursed lips in curiosity. As if she were one to judge. And then there was Zach, silently clapping in the background. Of course.

"Nice of you both to finally join us," Erin said, struggling to hold back her giggling. "We've already had our breakfast. We were too hungry to wait for you to, um, well, finish."

Kate shared an embarrassed look with me. I tried to think of a way out of this situation. She recovered first.

"I'll be back," she said, not looking back as she raced toward the shower block and abandoned me.

I took up a seat next to Zach. He was grinning at me the whole way.

"So did you get my little care package?" he leant in and whispered to me once I had sat down.

"Yeah, they weren't necessary though."

"You telling me you brought your own?" He looked at me incredulously. "You lie."

I shook my head.

"No? You don't want little shitlings running around do you? Because that's how you get little shitlings."

"No, no. We didn't… well… We didn't go that far."

He looked back and forth between the tent and I, confused.

"It certainly sounded like it," he whispered.

I turned crimson.

"What the hell were you doing in there then? Wait. Don't answer that. I don't actually want to know." He laughed hard at my embarrassed reaction.

"You want them back?"

He shook his head, laughing the whole time.

"You should keep them. You might need them later."

"I don't think…."

He patted me on the shoulder and interrupted me.

"You probably should," he said, laughing.

I let the conversation end there. I liked where things had gotten to and I was quite happy for them to stay there for a while. Though I'm sure he'd tell me

I was missing out. Frankly, I didn't care. Things were good.

Except for the sun. The sun was not good. The sun was not my friend. How had it gotten so damn bright? I was seriously regretting leaving the tent. My eyes seemed to be slowly drilling their way into the back of my head while my brain seemed to beat in time with my heartbeat, crushing itself against my skull in some vain attempt to escape from the poison I had suffered upon it. I covered my head with one of the blankets and hid until Kate returned.

I wasn't sure if I had fallen asleep or had simply tuned out completely, but a massive weight landed on my back suddenly and ripped me out of wherever I was, knocking the breath out of me.

"Come on sleepy head, go get ready, I want to go," Kate's muffled voice came through the blanket.

I grumbled a response. She countered by pulling the blanket off me. The sun was still not my friend. And my head was seriously questioning whether she was shoving me back into its cruel embrace on purpose.

I headed to the showers a second time, with shoes this time, and accepted the icy water quietly. For the throbbing in my head, it seemed like deserved punishment.

Thursday Afternoon January 1st 1998

"Hey Amy, I don't know about you, but I think it's time to start drinking again," Zach said with a grin. The colour instantly disappeared from her face and she twitched as if to throw up again. She took a deep breath, shook her head and curled in to ball.

"You bastard," Amy managed to mumble back.

Zach laughed.

"And what about you two?" he asked Kate and me. "You seem like you're ready to start again."

"Nah, we're ok," Kate responded, "this morning we're off looking for lyrebirds."

Zach stared at us blankly.

"Oh sure, 'looking for lyrebirds'. Of course we believe you," he said. "Well, you kids have fun. We'll just hang around here and entertain ourselves. And do come back this afternoon. I don't want to go out looking for you."

He had a point. Frankly, I wouldn't have believed our explanation either. Kate stood next to her car ready to leave. She had a backpack slung over shoulder and a large tourist map unfolded over the bonnet.

"Ignore him," Kate said to me. "Let's go."

"Where are we going, exactly?" I asked.

A fair question, I thought. While I had a little more faith in her and her honest desire to go bird watching than Zach did, at this stage she'd been deliberate vague. She traced what appeared to be the main highway carefully with her finger, mumbling to herself.

"I knew it was around here somewhere," she said excitedly.

She looked up with a half grin, flashed me a devious wink and folded up the map before I had a chance to see where we were going.

"You can be so confusing sometimes."

She poked her tongue out at me. "Yeah well, I'm a girl, you'll get used to it."

I hope not, I thought.

"Hold that thought," she said, touching my shoulder briefly. She turned and jumped into the driver's seat.

I only just gotten all my appendages into the passenger seat when she jammed the car into reverse and floored it. She was visibly excited. To see her so keen was cute. I found it infectious.

"Do you believe me now?" Kate asked.

I had to laugh, because if any place were going to have lyrebirds, it'd be the 'Lyre Bird Dell' walking track. She had me there. We'd parked at the top of a mountain; a tiny set of dirt stairs in front of us that quickly disappeared down a steep path walled in by thick bush that fell down the side of the mountain until it hit the unseen valley below. A sign told us it was an hour's walk to a natural pool below. Kate never bothered with the sign; she hit the path at a jog and never looked back, quickly slipping out of sight.

I finally caught up with her a good fifteen minutes later. She stood in the middle of the path, tense. One hand held her camera close to her face while the other pressed her lips to hush me. She held there, head cocked, listening patiently. Seconds ticked by. In the trees, a bird sung a high-pitched thrill and her fingers danced on the camera. The camera clicked thrice. Her shoulders slumped in disappointment.

"It wasn't one, was it?"

"I don't think so," she said with the shake of her head. "It was too hidden by the trees to get a decent shot, whatever it was."

224

We repeated this act twice more on the walk down, both times with the same conclusion. The forest surrounding the path down the mountain was too thick to see clearly through it. But the end, once the path opened into the lagoon at the bottom, was stunning. A stream of water fell a brief distance over a shadowy cave before hitting blackened rocks below. A modest pool formed the bottom of the waterfall before it continued on its way through the valley. The path ended there.

She kneeled at the water's edge and ran her fingers through the water.

"It's cold."

"What do we do now?" I asked.

She looked up at me. "Oh, I'm not close to giving up," she said, determined. "How do you feel about taking the less trodden path?"

I shrugged.

"Good answer."

What I'd really meant was I wasn't sure what she meant. She jumped up, grabbed my hand, lead me over the short wire fence that separated the publicly accessible area from the national forest and pulled me into the bushes. We stumbled through the thick scrub, down into the valley and up the other side. It never seemed like a good idea, to go crashing noisily through the bush looking for birds. Surely all the noise we were making was going to scare everything away.

And then a bird sang nearby. Serendipitous? Not quite. Close to perfect is never quite perfect enough. A façade over perfect. A flash of grey on the branch I happened to be looking at. The brown tail feathers identify it unequivocally. It was just... there, apparent and sat on a low branch directly in front of me.

"Look." I heard myself say, more reflex than intention. Time seemed slower than normal. My hand swung up to point her in the right direction. I was already slipping. I didn't notice, at first. All I saw was the brief flutter of grey wings as the bird took off in fright. Then my vision became a whole bunch of green blur.

We had been following a small ridgeline not far from where we'd first entered the bush when it happened. I didn't fall particularly far. That wasn't the issue. The issue was that thorny lantana covered the hill I slid down and the bottom was lined with rather jagged looking rocks. My face, thankfully, if one could be thankful in that moment, missed the rocks with but an inch to spare. My body, however, did not miss the lantana. As a side note: never go hiking in shorts again.

"Are you ok?" she called down to me.

"Sure."

That wasn't the complete truth. I picked myself up and brushed myself off. My legs were completely covered in tiny cuts. My shirt was torn. It stung everywhere. And the best part of it all was having to crawl back through the lantana to get back up again. This day was starting to hurt too much.

"Ouch?" she asked, rhetorically, once I'd made it back to the top. She stood in front of me, checking out all my scratches. "Maybe, perhaps this wasn't such a good idea?"

"I'll survive."

"Yes, I suppose you will," she said, rather cryptically.

"So did you see it?"

She shook her head.

"It was right there! Like, there there!" I tried all sorts of hand gestures to get across how close it was. All I managed to do was look like a crazy man all cut up and bleeding while waving his arms about.

"It's ok," she said with a gentle smile. "Let's head back to the water and get you cleaned up. This wasn't a great idea anyway."

"Sure it was a good idea. It simply didn't work out. And there's still plenty of sunlight left." I tried to reassure her.

"Maybe," she said, unconvinced.

We sat down on the pool's edge, side by side. She used the water to wash what she could. She tried to be soft. It didn't make much different. It hurt like hell. And it wasn't half as romantic as the movie tropes would leave one to believe such a moment should be. Her head tucked in low on my shoulder once she'd finished. In a way, it reminded me of how this all started.

And it gave me an idea. I lifted the camera from her, slipped the strap over her head and stood up. Her expression asked 'what the hell are you doing?'

I responded with a grin.

"Smile for me," I said.

Let this be said, I realise beauty may well be completely subjective, but my subject, as the camera focused on her gentle smile, was completely beautiful. The camera clicked. It didn't seem necessary. The image developed deep into my heart.

Still, a few more shots of film couldn't hurt.

"Enough," she said, laughing. "Film's expensive. Don't waste it on me."

She slipped in beside me, her arm wrapped around me and her head tucked in, held the camera out at arm's length with the lens pointed toward us.

"Smile for me," she said.

That I could do. I held her tightly. The camera clicked again. Only once more.

Her eyes drifted and the smile quietly left her behind.

"You know, this whole place brings back so many memories," she said. "I remember, Mum, Dad and I would go camping around here, a long, long time ago. Not here, here. But here in the Blue Mountains. Around when I was ten. Or maybe eleven? Something like that. There was a period back then when we used to come here every six months or so. It became the traditional Rees family holiday. I hated it, the camping stuff, but the one thing I always used to love was all the forest walks we'd go on. I'm pretty sure my love of birds started back then. There were always so many to see. I loved watching them and pointing out all the different kinds to Mum and Dad. Of course, we stopped not long after…"

She zoned out, lost momentarily in whatever memory had cut her off.

"It was different back then, life, you know," she half whispered. "I wish it was different now."

Her head sunk lower, further thoughts kept to herself.

"Are you disappointed about today?" I asked.

"No,"

"No? It's obvious that you are,"

"Do you love me?"

I wasn't ready for the question. Not delivered like that. One chance passed. Another soon slipped by. She drew in a breath. Respond, my mind screamed. One option left.

"Yes."

The truth. Nothing but. Love, loving her, I felt comfortable with that. I struggled with the answer, sure. But only because I couldn't wrap my mind wrapped around saying it. It wasn't something I'd given thought to; it had simply become my natural state of being. I breathed, I loved her. I breathed again.

Her eyes fluttered close. When they opened again, they were wet and rimmed red.

"You shouldn't," she whispered.

Maybe not, but I did, you silly girl.

Friday Morning January 16th 1998 ~ Today

"Love is like a wind stirring the grass beneath trees on a black night," he had said. *"You must not try to be definite and sure about it and to live beneath the trees, where soft night winds blow, the long hot day of disappointment comes swiftly and the gritty dust from passing wagons gathers upon lips inflamed and made tender by kisses."* – *Sherwood Anderson*, Winesburg, Ohio, *(1919), "Death"*

I want to tell you some fairy tale about how we lived happily ever after. I so desperately want to tell you how we lived happily ever after and rode off into the sunset or however else fairy tales are supposed to end. But it would be a lie. And I'm a terrible liar. Surely, moments aren't made to last forever.

She killed herself last week, on the morning of January 9th 1998. She was only 17. And I don't have a clue why. I don't have any answers. She didn't leave any. I keep searching and searching through my mind for answers. I'll never find any. All I know is that I loved her dearly. And now I don't know what to do. I want people to know her story. To know her like I knew her. The beautiful girl that showed me what the point of life is. And know the pain when that one guiding star in the dark night flickers out and leaves my world in darkness.

The funeral is today. I mean, her funeral is today. I don't even know how I got to today. I've been asked if I want to say something. I guess I'm supposed to. But say what? Somehow sum it all up, and somehow talk about everything in her I cared about. Stand up in front of all these people and somehow justify my existence in her life. They'll stare at me and wonder why I'm here and I will stare at them and wonder if they knew her how I knew her. But keep it short, there are others who needed the time to speak. And all I could think of was whether I was wearing too much black. Is too much wrong? There some protocol for this that I don't know. And I didn't know how to ask. Why the fuck does it matter what I wear? What fucking difference does it make now?

Mum drives us to the funeral. We're silent the entire way. She seems to know exactly the right thing to say. The sky is darkening and as we pull into the parking lot, a hastily written sign tells us that the service is to be held in the chapel. My body takes me along for the ride as it opens the car door, steps out and walks toward the funeral chapel.

There's a framed photo of her on an easel at the door. It looks like an old school photo, with her in her school uniform from at least a few years ago. She looks so young in the photo, cute. Amazing to think how much she'd grown up from this photo. God I miss her.

Inside, the funeral home seems mishandled. Cheap. Empty. Nothing in the room fits together; it was just a bunch of mismatched furniture dragged out to get through the service. Enough to make do. Bad music. Bad lighting. Balloons. Balloons, for fucks sake. This was all she was worth. Making do. That hurts.

The room is filled with people. I recognise faces from school. Most, I have no idea why they're here. How did they know Kate? Did they even? But they stare back at me as I walk down the aisle and I realise they're probably thinking the same thing. Two months ago, they'd have had a point. It'd only been two months. I can't believe that. Two halves of one life and her in the middle.

I pass by Zach and Erin, sitting toward the middle. Erin is bawling her eyes out on Zach's shoulder. I wasn't ready for them yet so I leave them be.

Nobody is sitting in the seat next to Amy so I choose it. She gives me a quick, resolute nod then leans her head against my shoulder. It's comforting. Then she goes back to staring at nothing. I join her.

The funeral director speaks for a while. A speech given emotionlessly into a barely comprehensible microphone, clearly delivered so many times before that it sounds rote and meaningless. I'm not paying attention. Instead, I watch the people around me as they listening to him, taking in all that empty bullshit.

An aunt speaks next, then a cousin and then the school captain. Each speech is as vapid and empty as the previous. Songs, apparently chosen from her favourite music, fill in each break in the diaphanous grief. Perhaps this tasteless pop might once have been her favourite, many years ago. But none of it sounds like the music she told me she liked. Did none of these people know who she was?

Then her father gets up to speak. He leans against the podium and takes a moment to compose himself. He speaks, first, of losing her mother and now her, his only child. He delivers it all so dispassionately that it sickens me. Amy takes my hand as he talks and squeezes hard enough to hurt. She stares forward blankly. I too wonder what part he had to play in this. And everything he says is all so clearly false that I

234

want to scream at him. Scream at them all. All they've spoken to is the masquerade she'd used to hide from them. Not one of them talks about her, the real her.

And now they expect me to add to her story. How do they expect me to do that? To tell her story? And not leave out the things that were important? All of it seemed important to me. How are you supposed to cut up a person's life? Do they even care? Would they understand? I doubt it.

I stand up, walk to the podium and look out at them. Everyone seems so… false. Fake, fake people with fake, fake sadness.

My fingers fumble with the bullet in my pocket and the memory of our first moments together come flooding back. I wish I could take them all away. Why couldn't I save you again? I'd trade every memory it brought for another moment with her.

I stand at the podium. Words come out. I can't tell you what. The words disappear as soon as their eyes steal them. I try to say what they expect me to say. I try to sound deep and meaningful. Profound even. I rattle off quotes about love and life that I researched because that's what people do in these situations. Whatever. That's what I'm sure they expect of me. What does that say about me? I sat down. And that is that. My contribution to her life. And from that moment, I knew that it would be forever inadequate.

There is a darkness that presupposes every question we humans ask, a quiet fear that not every question brings with it an answer. This is our original sin, the inevitable yearning for answers that takes us beyond the path our innocence can bear. I want my innocence back. Please bring her back.

Then the event is over, and everyone shuffles out so the venue can be recycled for the next dead person. Outside, the sky has gone dark, tumultuous, a reflection of my thoughts. I struggle to meet their faces, each of them watching me, and I can tell they're expecting me to act differently, to show some emotion. But I can't. I can't find them.

Lizzie finds me at the door, staring at Kate's photo. She wraps her arms around me and cries into my shoulder. I try my best to reciprocate. I try and I try but it doesn't seem to work. She gifts me an understanding look and hugs tighter.

"That was nice," Mum says, joining us.

Nice? How the fuck can a funeral be nice? I know she meant well but it hurts to reduce this down to such a simple word. And I want to fight back against it, but I can't find the words. So my thoughts curl up and hide away.

"I suppose."

Mum tried following it up with a supportive smile. She means well, I tell myself.

"I thought so too," Lizzie said.

"Me too," Zach added, wandering up to us with Erin.

As expected, there is an awkward apprehension between Lizzie and Zach, holding them apart. And the rest of us watch on, wondering what will happen next. Lizzie takes the first step, Zach, the second and in moments Lizzie is crying against his shoulder, whatever tension between them lost to the shared grief.

"What do you want to do now?" Mum asks.

What I want to do is jump into a time machine and go back in time a week to stop this from ever have happening. Can you give me that?

"We're thinking of heading back to Erin's, spend the afternoon with friends and relax. Will you join us Sam?" Zach said before I could answer.

"No, I think I'll stay a while. I'll find my own way home."

"Will you join us later?" Zach asks.

"Maybe. I'm not sure."

"Ok dude," he replies. "Remember we're here for you."

I know. But they're not what I need right now.

Amy finds me sheltering under the tin roof of the outdoor entrance to the chapel, leaning against one of the steel posts as the rain starts coming down. We stand and watch each other. I wasn't crying. Neither was she. The sky wept, but for Kate? That seemed too much to hope for. Amy seemed to understand. How false, the idea, as if crying were the only way to grieve. I feel so sick people of telling me how strong I am being. And others, constantly expounding how I don't need to be strong anymore.

There were no answers and there would never be answers, and the fear that brought is crushing me. We aren't ok. That's all there is to it. And that's ok. Amy understood, I think. I felt like she did. I need her. She needs me. We know it. Stuck together. We had to. As if only we understood.

She took out a manila folder and tentatively handed me a small stack of photos.

"I went around to her place a few days ago. Her dad asked me. Asked me if I wanted to take anything, you know, as a memento or something. I couldn't bring myself to spend long there. Too hard. But I grabbed her camera and I had the film developed. I think she would've wanted you to have them."

"I miss her," I say, taking the folder from her.

"Me too," she whispers, her bottom lip trembling.

I open the folder. And break down. The photos are all the ones I'd taken of Kate on our last trip together. Captured beauty. But the photos will never do her justice. How can you capture somebody's beauty in a picture? Certainly not hers. Her final lesson was the hardest.

There was one crucial photo missing. And it always would be. Because some birds aren't meant to be kept in cages. The lyrebirds. I understood, now, the façade Kate always presented. Too late. She was never searching for the birds, of course. She was only looking for somebody who could help her find her voice. Someone who understood what it meant to spend so long singing another's song that you forgot the sound of your own voice.

Did you not think I would listen? Maybe you didn't think so, but I would have, you silly girl. Your voice was beautiful and now I'll never hear you sing again.

Amy wraps her arms around me, burying her head into my chest.

"What happens now?" her broken voice asks.

"I really don't know."

And I didn't.

"Will you come somewhere with me?" I ask her. "I want to take you somewhere special."

It wasn't mine anymore.

Author's Notes

So now having reached this point, how did we get here? And why end it like that? Because...

So the story came to me, while I was in the shower of all places, as two sides to the same coin. A beginning and an end.

What if he saved her?

What if he didn't?

From that, I decided to take the narrator on a journey. To fall for a beautiful girl. To discover she wasn't as perfect as she seemed from the outside. To tear apart his perfect. And finally, to realise that she can give him so much more than perfect could. And with that, I stepped out of the shower knowing immediately that her story needed to be told.

In case there's doubt, Kate, Sam, Erin, Zach and all other characters never existed. This isn't an autobiography. Or a biography. The 90's Australia setting of this story came from the humorous 'discussions' I had between my editing friend

Schwartzie and me during the process of editing Crimson (my previous novel) and her constant berating of me about the 90's Australian colloquiums that keep creeping into my narrative. I thought I'd show her by setting the next story in 90's Australia and force the issue!

There are little things stolen from my life to fill out the narrative, where I felt they didn't have material adverse effect on the plot or characters:

I really had a border collie, though it was a he and he was far lazier.

I really did live in a half-renovated set of flats, though I never had an awesome projector setup.

I really used to go jumping off the sand cliffs of a nearby beach, though 'cliffs' in this instance measure not more than a metre or so.

I still lament the disappearance of Jolt Cola, a staple of my formative years.

Capsicum isn't food.

And, of course, Jurassic Park is still the best movie ever, no caveats necessary.

You're probably wondering why? Why'd she do it? Why end the story like that?

Unfortunately, even here, as I wrote for Sam, there are no answers. I've been intentionally vague, to the point that though I've dropped 'hints' throughout the story, the reality is that even internally I've never explored them. I didn't want to. I kept myself in the dark to ensure that Sam's narrative reflected the uncertainty he felt. What was her father's part in the story? Do Sam and Amy end up together? What happened in the days leading up to her choosing to take her life? No idea. I don't have the answers. You're allowed to be annoyed at that.

It's a tough subject, suicide. And it always leaves questions that will never have answers.